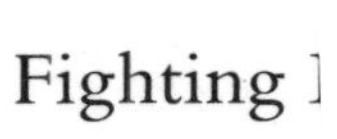
Fighting

CW01081892

ALSO BY CLAUDE GUTMAN

The Empty House

CLAUDE GUTMAN

Fighting Back

Translated from the French by
ANTHEA BELL

TURTON & CHAMBERS

First published in France by
Éditions Gallimard, Paris
under the title *L'Hôtel du retour*

First published in England and Australia 1992

Turton & Chambers Ltd
Station Road, Woodchester
Stroud, Glos GL5 5EQ, England
and 10 Armagh Street
Victoria Park, Perth
Western Australia 6100

Typeset by Avonset, Midsomer Norton, Bath
Printed by SRP, Exeter

Cataloguing in Publication Data
available from the British Library

ISBN 1 872148 75 1

For my father.
For Lajzar Gutman
and Freida Stirboul,
the grandparents I never knew.

To Montreuil-sous-Bois,
the town of my memories.

IT wasn't until much later that I discovered what the Nazis had done with Lonia, Maurice, Hanna, the twins, little Perla, Ida, Rachel, Samuel and Hélène. They'd been herded into a tarpaulin-covered lorry one day when I wasn't there. They were all I had in the world, and the Gestapo had taken them away from me. They were driven to the railway station in the town of G., loaded into a cattle truck, and then the train moved away.

I cried, howled, kicked trees, refused the meals Monsieur Rigal, the local policeman, took me, prayed for the children to be brought back; it did no good at all. I was alone, and condemned to remain alive.

Monsieur Rigal was anxious about me, and wouldn't leave my side. He came and stayed with me in the big, empty house. As he followed me about he kept repeating that there was no reason for me to go on living there. He watched me tidy up the dormitory where the little ones had slept, make their beds, put dolls back in their proper places, polish Lonia's desk the way I'd watched her do it every day. I had no tears left in me. I couldn't cry any more, but I couldn't laugh. Monsieur Rigal wanted to help me, but I wouldn't let him. The empty house was mine. No one else had the right to touch it. I swept all the rooms. I washed the kitchen floor, and I looked into Monsieur Rigal's eyes. What I saw there was fear.

I knew he wanted to hug me, comfort me and help me, but there was nothing he could do that would ease my pain. Yet I could still do something for him; I could rid him of his fear that I'd do 'something stupid'. That was the last thing he'd said before I retreated into silence.

Two days later, when I found that all the knives had disappeared from the big cutlery drawer in the kitchen, I knew what he meant by 'something stupid'. I went over to tall, gruff Monsieur Rigal, took his hand, led him to the dining room and made him sit down. I went over to the piano. I took the photograph of my parents out of my back pocket and put it on the music holder. Then I played four bars of a Chopin waltz and turned to him again.

'I'm going to find them, Monsieur Rigal. I'm not going to do anything "stupid". You can put the knives back in the kitchen.'

And I saw him shed real tears of joy, sitting there with his head in his hands. He had to mop his face with his big checked handkerchief. Then he stood up and put his arms around me, lifting me right off the ground even though I was fifteen years old. His moustache scrubbed my cheeks.

'You had me really frightened, David!'

I closed the piano lid, put the photograph back in my pocket, took his hand again, and went round the whole place for the last time, visiting every room. Then I shut the front door behind us, and we walked off into the grounds without looking back.

Monsieur Rigal knew that he could take me home with him now.

Halfway to his house, I realized he was still holding my hand. I took it away. Holding hands felt silly at my age. Monsieur Rigal understood. He let me walk on at my own pace, independent. There was nothing I'd wanted to take from the house. Just before leaving I had picked a flower from the garden and put it on Lonia's desk, that was all. If she ever came back she'd know who had left it there.

At the crossroads where the path through the grounds and the main road met, Monsieur Rigal put his hand on my shoulder. I jerked away quite violently, but I was grateful all the same. He was helping me to face the memory of that bright early morning when I came up the road on my bicycle, cycling back and forth in zigzags because I was so happy after spending the night with my girlfriend Claire, and he jumped out to prevent me falling into the clutches of the SS. We stopped, just for a second.

Walking a few paces behind him, I wiped my face

with the back of my sleeve. Lonia, Maurice, Hanna and the others had all gone away down the road leading to G. I took the road to the village.

Opening the door of his home, Monsieur Rigal asked me not to mind the untidiness; he'd soon put things straight. He opened the shutters of the kitchen window a little way and pointed to a chair.

'I'll be back in a minute or so. The wife's not here. I sent her to see her old aunt.'

What had that to do with me? I watched him go down the steps to his cellar.

As I waited, I gazed at several flies in their death throes, stuck to the flypaper dangling from the ceiling light above the table. They made a horrible noise. There would be a sudden silence, and then another fly would start fighting for its life.

Monsieur Rigal's voice floated up from the cellar. He was humming cheerfully.

I didn't want to stay in the kitchen. The flypaper disgusted me.

I pushed the shutters as wide as they would go to air the room. I leaned my elbows on the windowsill.

My new horizon. The squat black church on the other side of the road, its porch blocked from my view by the war memorial with the long list of names carved on grey marble. Monsieur Rigal was still humming. The surname Rigal appeared on the monument four times. I deciphered the first names: Jules, Henri, Joseph and Pierre. 'Died for France', said the carved words, and the happy song

Monsieur Rigal was humming went round and round in my head.

He shouldn't be doing it. I couldn't tear my eyes from those names. I clutched the windowsill. The cellar door slammed, bringing me back to reality. But Monsieur Rigal shouldn't be singing. Jules, Henri, Joseph and Pierre, who had all 'died for France'.

Lonia, Maurice, Hanna, the twins, little Perla, Ida, Rachel, Samuel and Hélène . . . they'd have died for nothing.

'We must drink to this, lad!' cried Monsieur Rigal, a bottle in his hand.

I went on staring out of the window.

'What is it, David?'

I could sense his presence behind me. I knew that he was looking at the war memorial. The soldier sculpted in stone was looking ahead, gallant and unafraid. I heard Monsieur Rigal's heavy tread moving towards the table with the frayed oilcloth cover. He put the bottle down.

'We'll drink to it another time.'

He stood beside me, shoulder to shoulder. We were both looking at the memorial to the dead of the Great War, a monument erected by a grateful country.

'Jules, well . . . he was my father. The others . . . they're my brothers. That what you wanted to know? I was the youngest.'

His words came out in fits and starts.

'Got sent to the Front myself. Right at the end,

that was. The only survivor. My name will never be on that stone. And to tell you the truth, if I could knock it down . . . ' He was close to me again. 'Sole survivor, that's me.'

But I didn't really care about the letters the police brought Monsieur Rigal's mother, the medals and the funerals and all the tears. I really didn't care about the pressure of his shoulder against mine as he tried to help me understand the horror of that war, trenches and fixed bayonets and mud, men's friends ripped open and dying before their eyes, their officers hanging back, all the ugliness of it. Because I was thinking of my parents and how *I* was going to find them again, that's what I was going to do.

As he talked about his dead family I thought of my living one. I heard him offer good advice and curse the Germans, explaining that they were still around, quite close to the village, and though they were in retreat they were still killing and looting. He told me how they'd shut up all the people of Oradour-sur-Glane in their village church and then set fire to it. How they'd hanged hostages from balconies and street lamps in Tulle. He kept on and on about the German forces in France. The idea was for me to follow him down those paths of hatred and vengeance, but I just let his talk of barbarity, blood and atrocities wash over me as I thought of how Mother would smile when she saw me again.

Suddenly I was brought back to earth.

'Now, you mustn't go out of the house for four or five days,' he was saying. 'It's too risky. I'll explain.'

I lifted my head and looked him straight in the eye. He must have seen more hatred in my face than any he felt for the Germans. As if I could still be told what to do! As if anyone had any kind of authority over me! My life was mine, *mine*, now! My childhood was gone, and I no longer felt inclined to obey other people's orders. What I had to do now was look after myself, find my parents, and forget those dead children.

'It's for your own good, David.'

Yes, and he'd already done plenty 'for my own good', hadn't he? Monsieur Rigal might have saved my life, but would a whole lifetime be long enough to exhaust my regrets that I hadn't gone away in the Gestapo's tarpaulin-covered lorry?

Monsieur Rigal looked at me oddly, baffled.

My own good? Oh, terrific! There were a lot of people who'd done what they could for my own good. All that effort, just for me to end up six hundred kilometres from my home in Paris, in the kitchen of an old country policeman who wanted to boss me around.

My own good? What did they know about it? What had anyone ever known about it? I'd been running away, always on the run. First to escape the French police who arrested my parents. Then hiding under false names to slip out of the clutches of the Germans. Only a shadow of myself, keeping my head down, never raising my voice . . . and all that just to see everyone I loved taken away.

Monsieur Rigal had misunderstood my silence

during the short time he'd spent with me in the empty house, keeping an eye on me. He'd respected my grief, thinking in his simple-minded way that he could make me do what he thought best and carry on acting for 'my own good'.

So for a start he was telling me I couldn't go out, not for several days, just like that. Nothing doing!

'I'll go out if I like,' I said.

Turning away from the window, I took a couple of steps towards the door.

At this point I had a shock, because my anger at the idea of being kept prisoner was matched by Monsieur Rigal's sudden fury. He gripped my arm so hard that it hurt, turned me around and hit me hard with his free hand, holding my arm tighter than ever to keep me from falling. For a moment I must have felt faint, because next thing I knew I was sitting opposite him with my elbows on the table.

'Bloody little idiot!' was the first thing I heard. Monsieur Rigal put a glass of wine in front of me.

'Drink that. Should help you collect your thoughts.'

I drained the glass.

Monsieur Rigal laughed. 'Like another, you pig-headed little idiot?'

He held out his own glass, and I reluctantly clinked mine against it. The old soak! I'd always been rather scared of him when he'd been drinking.

Lonia, oddly enough, thought highly of him. Whenever he came to the house, she would give him something to eat or drink and then they would go into her office and talk.

I glanced sideways at Monsieur Rigal.

'Sorry I called you a little idiot, lad. You deserved what you got, though.'

His usual good-natured, ponderous manner was entirely gone now.

'I've got very good reasons for making you stay indoors, see? Know about the Maquis, do you?'

Just what did this big bruiser think he could teach me? Mister Plod the policeman!

Well, of course I knew about the Maquis. I nodded.

'No, you don't, lad. You don't know the first thing about them, specially not just now.'

In spite of my resentment and my wish to escape I found myself sitting there frowning, one hand over my mouth, while I became a small boy listening to a bedtime story. But the story Monsieur Rigal told, in all its detail, was even nastier than *Bluebeard*.

'There's bright lads like you in the woods all over the place, older ones too; the whole region's full of them. They thought they could see the Germans off with their popguns. They didn't mind what they did – right, the Germans may be on the run, but it's no use thinking random strikes will dislodge them just like that! No use firing on the first convoy to pass, then going home to take cover. Which is what they did, poor fools, a couple of days before those dirty Boches came to pick you all up at the children's home. Reprisals, understand?'

I didn't just yet, or not very well, but I saw Monsieur Rigal's eyes grow sad.

What happened in the village then was sheer butchery.

'I told them to shelter somewhere else. But I was just a silly old man, wasn't I? Well, sure enough, the SS came back. In the morning, while you were at school, David. Luckily for me, I was . . .'

He stopped for a moment. This was where the horror began.

'They made straight for the farms, the bakery, the grocer's shop and the bar. They drove the little children out of doors, hitting them with sticks. If I could get my hands on the bastard who denounced them . . . '

Monsieur Rigal had raised his voice. He slammed his fist down on the table, breaking his glass and not even noticing the wine spilling over the oilcloth. I knew how he felt. I'd have liked to get my hands on the bastard who denounced them myself.

There was a long silence. We sat there, each absorbed in his own hatred. Looking into Monsieur Rigal's eyes, I could see the victims filing past, and the revenge he'd have liked to take on their executioners.

'You should have seen them, David. Bruised and battered, hands tied behind their backs. Pierrette, the baker's wife, she couldn't even walk. They summoned all the village together with their loudspeakers. They lined their victims up behind the church. Then they just shot them down and left them lying there in their own blood. They got back into their armoured cars and drove off – and there we stood, the whole village, couldn't move, couldn't speak, like a lot of graven images, until Pierrot's mother started screaming. Gone off her head.'

Monsieur Rigal swallowed, with difficulty.

'That's why you have to keep quiet, David.'

But I knew he was thinking what I was thinking. Someone there, watching the execution, was the person who had denounced the Maquis.

'That'll do for now.'

Monsieur Rigal could bear no more. Nor could I. But neither of us was going to give way.

He rose to his feet.

'Get you something to eat.'

An excuse: anything to drive out the pictures in his mind's eye.

He went over to the kitchen dresser, opened a drawer, closed it again, picked up a pan out of the sink, put it down. Then came back to me. I hadn't moved from my chair. I sat there looking at the puddles of wine on the table. He patted my head with his big hand.

'Don't hold it against me, do you?'

He couldn't see my face, or the single tear running down my cheek.

Nor could he have guessed anything more over the next two nights, which I spent alone in my new bedroom. Yet another new bedroom, no more mine than anyone else's, really. I was like a piece of left luggage being moved from place to place. Even though I was worn out, I couldn't sleep. I wanted to sink into the high bed with its eiderdown, bury my head in the feather pillow and never wake up again. I wanted to sleep there for ever, drift away to join the friends I'd abandoned. They'd never forgive me. I crushed my face against the pillow and tried to get some rest, but all I got was the long nightmare of a tarpaulin-covered lorry driving away without me.

Wearing a silly nightshirt, much too big for me, I tried not to make the bedstead creak.

Monsieur Rigal must be asleep next door. I sat up, got out of bed, went back to bed, got out again. I lit the candle on my bedside table. I looked at my parents' photograph over and over again. I thought about them, hard. Would they recognize me? I walked about the room on tiptoe. I went back to bed again. I blew the candle out and then relit it. I kissed the photograph of my father and my mother. I looked at their eyes, which seemed to speak to me. I remembered those two pairs of eyes looking up at the window to see me for the last time, the day of the big raid to round up Jews. Two pairs of eyes with a look in them that went right through me. I doubled up with pain. Lying on the floor, I clutched the photograph as tightly as I could. Oh, Mother, Father, I swore, I'll find you. I started repeating those words to myself, clenching my fist so hard that my nails lacerated the palm of my hand. There was no way I could calm down, no way the pains in my stomach would stop. And the tears wouldn't come.

How long ago had Monsieur Rigal sent me to bed? What time would it be now? I was aware only of the clammy heat. I opened the shutters. It was a starlit night, and a warm breeze blew into the dark little room once more. I closed the shutters and started prowling round my room. The candle did me no good now. I might be used to the dark but I wasn't used to pain yet. I could recognize it, that was all, and the pain tormenting me now was almost driving me mad. My lost parents, my friends who'd been taken away, all those dead people Monsieur Rigal had been talking about came to torment me. They weren't just numbers, they were human corpses watching me, pointing at me, asking, 'Why aren't you dead too?' I woke with a start.

I was sitting up leaning against the leg of the bed, facing the wardrobe. My nightmare had woken me. I felt cold, although my nightshirt was wringing wet. Arms flailing, I pushed all the dead people away from me. Monsieur Rigal! Monsieur Rigal was the only person who could do anything about it. I might be grown up now and ready to take on the whole world, but there was still a very little boy inside me, almost a baby, urging me to find a friendly soul to calm my fears.

I groped my way to the landing. There was a faint light in Monsieur Rigal's bedroom. I heard whispering too. The crazy old boy must be talking to himself. Never mind. I didn't knock. I had to find refuge in his arms. When I pushed the door it opened easily.

I'm not sure how many of them were sitting on the floor, startled, snatching up the guns lying beside them. What I remember most is how ashamed I felt of bursting in like that. I was paralysed by terror at the sudden silence I'd caused. And I'd been going to beg for a little kindness . . . I turned and ran back to bed, colliding with all sorts of things on the way, until I was lying stupefied with tears on the high bed which squealed every time I hiccupped. Over the past two years, when so many horrible things had happened to me, I'd only been able to squeeze the tears out in driblets. Now I was suddenly making up for lost time, weeping the sort of tears anyone can shed at any age. Tears of fury and relief. It was good to feel my violence ebbing away. Through the mists around me I heard the reassuring footsteps of Monsieur Rigal coming to help me. I'd got what I wanted. My pain receded as he stroked my shoulders, my back, my head with his big warm hands.

I don't remember what he said, but it was enough. It was like a gentle tune lulling an unhappy child to sleep.

Next morning, when I came downstairs in my nightshirt, which looked as silly as ever, the resentment that had left me just for that one night flared up again.

Monsieur Rigal was slowly drinking something he had the nerve to call coffee. He looked at me surreptitiously, smiling. I had nothing but anger to offer in reply.

'Well, thanks a lot for all the secrecy, not to mention the moral lessons about taking precautions.'

He sat there with his cup halfway to his lips, looking as if he might throw it in my face. But he controlled himself.

'There's some things are really urgent, lad.'

'Like knowing the raid on the home was going to happen – you being so well informed, after all – and not managing to save anyone but me. None of the others. That's horrible. Really horrible.'

'But I didn't know about the raid, David.'

'Liar. You're a liar. You're a bastard. Where are they now? Tell me where they are!'

'Take it easy, David, lad. Calm down.'

'I can't stand it here in this hole! I have to do something! Anything! I'm sick of this, absolutely sick of it! I want to fight. I don't care about dying. I want to kill them, to slaughter them, murder the swine who took them away from me – who took . . .'

But I couldn't utter the names of all the dear people I'd lost. I stood there trembling, shaken by what Lonia used to call a fit of nerves when Maurice began shouting in the middle of a meal, fighting his own private ghosts. She used to shoo the rest of us away. Lonia knew what to do, knew the words to calm him.

Monsieur Rigal put his cup down. He came over to me and stood there for a long, long time running his hand over my hair, promising me they'd all be avenged but saying patience was needed. Just a little patience. Yes, the Allies had landed, and yes, the Germans were retreating, but we mustn't take risks.

'That would just be stupid, see?'

I nodded submissively. I drank my so-called coffee and went back to my bedroom.

The war memorial still stood there, challenging me. And there sat Monsieur Rigal downstairs, so certain he'd brought me to heel, while I was up here in my little cell, pacing from wall to wall, from the bed to the wardrobe, from the window to the door, from the door to the window. Another glance at the war memorial. The whole thing was nauseating.

Lying on my bed, I supposed all I had to do was wait for the war to end, whereupon Monsieur Rigal would knock on the door and announce, 'There, it's all over. You can come out of hiding now.'

The thought was so ridiculous, I smiled. In the middle of planning fearful vengeance, I jumped as I heard the front door close. Looking out of the window, I saw Monsieur Rigal riding away on his bike. I found myself waving goodbye.

Goodbye, Monsieur Rigal. You did your best, but I'm going my own way now. Maybe we'll meet again one day.

Love, David.

What would he do? What would he say when he found my brief note on the kitchen table? I could have written a long, long letter of apologies and thanks, but that's how it came out. 'I'm going my own way now.' Other people weren't going to make any more decisions for me.

I walked slowly out of the village. It was fine warm weather. I began whistling to keep my spirits up. Monsieur Rigal thought of me as a child, but I'd had enough of people feeling sorry for me. And in the end, well, life was going to be good!

I'd never taken so much notice of this road before. Crops of wheat, maize, tobacco: as far as I was concerned they might not have existed at all for these last two years of wartime. I'd been skulking around on the outskirts of life, looking at the ground. Well, that was all over. I was going to walk with my head held high. And so I did until I reached the minor road leading to the empty house. Then I began sweating, I felt frightened, and cold, and my certainties melted away. For a moment I felt dizzy, and then my anger was back again.

I began running through the undergrowth. I wanted to see the empty house again, find the evidence that all I'd been through was true, and I was still alive in spite of myself.

I climbed the steps to the front door four at a time. I pushed the door open, knowing there was no one waiting for me inside. I caressed the piano in the dining room. Then I went up to the boys' dormitory, where I sat on my bed with my head in my hands.

I found a lost sock under Samuel's bed and put it away. One sock: all that was left of a small boy of ten.

Little Samuel. He never said a word to me, not one, not part of one. I didn't discover his existence at all until the second day after my arrival, the day I found the piano. He was curled up on the floor in a corner, like a dog, his own corner of the dining room. I saw his lifeless face, his big empty eyes which had seen too many horrors. He was breathing, but he was absolutely still until the moment when the first notes sounded. I was too busy looking where I put my fingers to see him uncurl himself and come over to stand very close against me. His eyes were trying to tell me something, something so important that I was frightened and took no notice of anything but the black and white keys while he laid his head against my shoulder. When I had struck the last chord I watched him walk stiffly back to his corner, shaken to the core.

Who was looking after little Samuel now? Who was dressing and undressing him, while he gave no sign of feeling anything? Who was tucking him up in bed and singing him to sleep; who was making his eyes look as if they'd like to speak?

Sitting there looking at his bed, I thought: I love you, little Samuel. It's as if you were still here, and

I was still trying to get you to talk.

I'd spent three days in that house after *they* threw all my friends into their tarpaulin-covered lorry. Three days thinking of nothing but myself. Why was I the one left on my own? What injustice had kept me out of the cattle truck carrying all the others into the unknown? Monsieur Rigal had told me what happened to them at the station. I'd have helped Lonia. I'd have helped them all. They'd have helped me. And here and now, sitting on my bed in this room which I supposed they'd never see again, I wouldn't have had to picture them as they used to be, singing and crying and scuffling. Little Samuel.

I thought: why not set this dreadful house on fire, destroy everything, obliterate it? What was the use of cupboards full of the children's things, their smell, their lives, if the children themselves were never coming back?

I stood up, furiously angry, and set about the work of destruction. Everything I had lovingly, painstakingly and pointlessly tidied up became the target of my fury. I overturned the beds, kicked blankets about, flung open cupboard doors and sent pullovers, trousers and underwear flying.

I opened bedside tables, uncovering their small secrets, lucky mascots for unhappy children: pine cones picked up during our walks, photographs, treasured little bits of ribbon. I don't think there's any name for the frenzy I indulged in, unashamed, or the regret that came over me just as suddenly.

I went down to Lonia's office and crumpled up

her map of Europe with the tiny flags on it. I tipped over the glass of water, tore the flower to pieces and scuffed the polished floor. Then I went back up to the dormitory as fast as I'd run down. It was in a terrible mess. I threw myself on the floor, hugging the sheets and blankets, rolling about in the smell of my friends who had gone. *They*, the Germans, had had no right to take them away – no right at all.

No more than I had any right to destroy the few things to which they'd clung to help them survive.

Suppose someone had done the same thing to me?

Frantically I tidied everything away again: Maurice's blue scarf, the toy boat I'd carved for Nathan. Then I went out into the grounds to look for my hiding place, my shoe box with Claire's letters in it: my own little treasures, all I had.

Claire. She was the only person who might be able to help me. Unless – no, that wasn't possible. She surely couldn't be angry with me, but I ought to have told her what was happening. I'd let a whole week go by without sending any news. Oh Claire, I thought, I'm sorry. I was thinking of her so much that I'd been going to her when I left the shelter of Monsieur Rigal's house. I ran away from him for your sake, Claire, I thought. I love you; you can't not love me. Say so, Claire, tell me you love me and you don't regret anything that happened.

Sitting on the grass with the open shoe box, I took out Claire's letters one by one. There was no point in what I was doing. I knew them by heart: the letters I'd waited for so anxiously, letters about her love or her doubts. Spread out in front of me, they brought back sudden, unexpected memories. I'd read that particular letter in the little wood beside the bend in the road. I'd read this one surreptitiously in the classroom, with its smell of chalk and polish, the night I got out of bed and came down to answer it. This one was a letter apologizing for a meeting she'd missed: it revived hope in me after uncertainty.

But as I read, the letters suddenly became nothing but sheets of paper covered with meaningless words – just rubbish to be thrown away. Nothing mattered any more. My shoe box was only a shoe box, and the words I was reading out loud were just words, pointlessly strung together, listed like entries in a dictionary. Yet they'd once inspired me with anguish, torment and delight. Why did they no longer excite me? At random I unfolded a letter which had once been my special treasure.

I remember the sweetness of your skin
Your glance
Your voice.
Through these endless days
I think of all we could be sharing
If we were together.

The paper hung from my fingers. After what had happened could there still be any power in those words?

Images danced in front of my eyes. I lay down on the grass. *Your skin, your glance, your voice . . . together.*

I sat up again. The words I knew by heart had revived me after all. Now I have nothing left but you, Claire, I thought. Will you still want me? For a split second I saw her face. Only a few minutes and we'd be together again.

I ran towards the house with my shoe box under my arm, stuffed it into a canvas bag with a few other things, and took all the money and ration cards I could find. I felt no shame in stealing. Then I took the bicycle that had belonged to Madame Salviac the cook and I left the empty house for good.

I have never cycled to G. so fast before. I had no time to waste on self-pity: memories threatened to come back with every turn of the pedals. I had to stamp on my feelings, kill them, forbid them to come to life or I'd have been stopping to deal with them every metre or so. I had to build a dam, but one flick of the finger and it would burst. Too bad. I had to get over the past, forget it. I just had to pedal and pedal, looking straight ahead, until G. and its church came in sight.

I had a suspicion that the town wasn't exactly the same as it used to be, although this was no more than a vague sensation because I was fully occupied cycling up the deceptive rise which led to the town walls, and then downhill again to Claire's house. No more taking care to hurry past her street in case her parents saw: all those silly childish worries were over. I was on my way to Claire. I'd ring the bell at the front door and the old housekeeper would come hobbling to open it. I'd push her aside to climb the stairs all the faster, and I'd see Claire's room for the first time. Oh, Claire! I'd fling my arms round her and sense her body, her skin, her perfume. She meant everything to me, whatever happened. And if by any chance her father was there and he dared open his mouth I wouldn't say a word, I'd just knock him down, I'd destroy him. Claire, Claire! Only one more left turn now. I braked as I cycled the last few metres. Her house.

The gate was bolted. The shutters were closed. The house was deserted; there was mail spilling out of the letter box.

I got off my bicycle in the middle of the road. Sitting cross-legged beside it, I stared at the house and never even heard the hooting of a lorry squealing to a halt, for what or for whom I had no idea. The surface of the road was warm, which hardly made up for the shout of, 'What the hell d'you think you're doing, you young idiot? Can't you see I want to get by?' The lorry driver slung me up on the pavement along with my bike, which fell against the iron railings outside the house. A door slammed, and the lorry drove on.

My knees were bleeding as I leant against the low wall beneath the railings. I heard almost none of the remarks of the passers-by who were wondering anxiously if I had lost my wits. All I remember is an exclamation of 'Poor child!' from a kindly woman in black who bent down to me, a baffled expression on her face.

'Sod the poor child!' I said. 'Piss off!'

Shocked, she walked away looking hurt. As a matter of fact I certainly didn't have all my wits about me, but she wasn't to know that.

And nobody could have known I was fed to the teeth with being a 'poor child'. In my distress I felt like spitting at them all. 'Poor child.' Was that all they could say, when they were the ones who'd made a 'poor child' of me? Adults and their filthy, foul, horrible war. I might be a 'poor child', but I'd never asked for any of it. It wasn't my decision, aged eleven, to incur the hostility of the Germans, wear the shameful yellow star and see my parents arrested. 'Poor child', taking refuge in a boarding school, then carted off to a Home for Jewish children, then seeing them all taken away. 'Poor child', indeed! I felt like saying 'Poor old folks' as I sat there with blood trickling from my knees. I wanted to howl insults back into their sympathetic faces. Poor, wretched oldies!

Well, enough. I wasn't going to be a 'poor child' any more.

I stood up and pulled the bell, though without any real hope, looking at the closed shutters of Claire's room, hardly able to believe she wasn't there. Suppose she actually did appear? But there wasn't any 'suppose' about it. Only my hand holding the chain that pulled the bell, and the bell itself ringing.

I was aware of ironic looks at a badly dressed teenager with his socks coming down, trying to rouse an absent household.

'Can't you see there isn't anyone at home?'

I didn't even bother to reply.

Claire must know what had happened! Surely my frantic ringing would get through to her somehow? Perhaps I was going mad myself?

I gave up. It was only another meeting missed.

I took my exercise book out of the canvas bag which I'd tied to the carrier of my bike with a bit of string, tore out a sheet, found a pencil and scribbled the most loving words I could think of, with my address in Paris. We'd see each other again. I folded my piece of paper in four and tucked it into the letter box with the rest of the mail.

Spitting on my handkerchief and scrubbing my legs with it, I tried to get rid of the marks of dried blood.

Claire's house looked beautiful in the midday sun as I cycled away from it, going somewhere else.

But where? I cycled round inside the walls three times, and still didn't know. Back to Monsieur Rigal? That would be admitting defeat. So I went round the walls a fourth time, in the shade of the sweet chestnut trees.

'Daniel! Daniel!'

I couldn't fail to recognize that voice. I braked. Monsieur Legendre came running up beside me. Obviously he could hardly believe it. He was feeling my arms, stroking my hands.

'Daniel! It really *is* you!'

Daniel Larcher was the false name I'd used for going to school in G.

'No. David. David Grunbaum. You must have made a mistake, sir!'

But I was smiling, and he hugged me, embracing me with tears in his eyes. I felt awkward, in full view of everyone, but it was good to see Monsieur Legendre again.

'It really is you! So you were the one who escaped the raid?'

What could I say? Here I was, wasn't I?

Whatever mechanism usually controlled Monsieur Legendre had been thrown right out of gear. He'd always been so reserved, almost severe, interested only in my fingering, my sharps and flats, my cadences and his metronome. Now he'd entirely lost his look of reserve and the gestures that were as restrained as his suit. This wasn't *my* Monsieur Legendre, my old piano teacher. This was a voluble, gesticulating Monsieur Legendre, embarking on a long diatribe against the bloody militia, those soldiers who were countrymen of mine and yet could use armed force against their own people to carry out German orders. Collaborators who all ought to be shot, screamed Monsieur Legendre, although that didn't prevent him looking at my hands, just checking to see if they might still be in a fit state to make me a future Rubinstein.

'Let me buy you a drink, Daniel.'

'Not Daniel, thanks, but David would like one.'

He smiled.

'Sorry, I can't get used to it.'

'I never could, either.'

*

We sat in front of the café, with the old town before us, and Monsieur Legendre invited me to stay with him until 'all this' was over. 'All this' meant the things he was now telling me. I only listened with half an ear after he told me about the hurried departure of Claire's family.

'She came in one day, gave me an envelope with money in it, and then she shook hands and went away. Very shy, she seemed. I was fond of young Claire.'

So Monsieur Legendre hadn't guessed about us. I hadn't just been fond of her, though, I loved her. My anger revived again.

Why, I wondered, why all this violence? And the executions Monsieur Legendre was talking about. The partisans had killed the owner of the café in the Avenue Gambetta, a collaborator. He'd been assassinated in broad daylight.

And a good thing too, I thought. I hoped they'd kill as many as possible of the bastards who had no qualms about denouncing me as a Jew, the filthy police who thought they had nothing to be ashamed of because they were only obeying orders.

Something Lonia had said came back to me.

'Always remember that the men who came for your parents weren't Germans, they were *French* policemen.' She rolled the 'r' of 'French'. It went right through me.

Right, so Lonia had told me to remember. She never told me to forgive them.

*

A boy from my class waved to me from a distance and went on his way. So far as he was concerned, nothing had happened. I'd been off school for several days, nothing to make a song and dance about, it was just an absence with an ordinary explanation. Maybe I'd had flu.

'Larcher, Daniel?'

'He's not here, sir.'

And my false name would have been entered in the 'Absent' column of the big register, which went round the school from hour to hour, class to class and day to day.

They'd all been getting on with their ordinary lives, at home with their mothers and fathers, who might occasionally throw a fit over a bad report for maths. That was life, and I ought to have accepted the unacceptable. Everyone for himself, in his own little cocoon, watching other people die. Buying food on the black market just to survive.

Monsieur Legendre gave me an odd glance.

'What's wrong?' I asked.

'Nothing. You look pale, that's all.'

He was right. I didn't feel well. In fact I felt sick with envy. Sick because I knew that, like the others, if I had my mother and father the world could have collapsed around my ears and I wouldn't have cared a bit. I was a rat. Being Jewish was no excuse. But their lives and mine were different. There were only a few kilometres between the empty house and this town, but it might as well have been an ocean.

And I'd rather have been like them. So who had decided otherwise? Lonia used to say that one day men would be masters of their fate. Well, I just hoped that day would hurry up and come.

Monsieur Legendre laid his hand on mine. That warm touch roused me from my thoughts.

'All right, Daniel?'

'David, Monsieur Legendre. I'm David for good now. You don't know what it's like, having to hide your own name and pretend to be somebody else all the time.'

'You must go on pretending, though – not for long, but you really must.'

I got up, about to walk away. I wanted to hurt him.

'Never again, Monsieur Legendre. Never again, understand?'

'What about the militia, and the Germans?'

'I want to see them in hell, as soon as possible, and I promise you I'll do all I can to help them on their way.'

'Listen, David, you really must stay in hiding. All right, things are moving fast now, but you don't know the whole story.'

'I know all I need to know, and I don't care.'

Suddenly Monsieur Legendre's hand came down violently on my forearm. He made me sit down again before I realized what the matter was. His voice was sharp.

'Keep your mouth shut.'

He had hardly spoken when six large uniformed

militiamen, led by a red-faced countryman about forty years old, marched into the café and brought out the waiter. He was dazed and bleeding from the scalp. They set about kicking and punching him in front of the customers, who sat there motionless outside the café. The fat, red-faced man gave us a contemptuous glance. He looked like Mussolini.

'That's what happens to Gaullist scum!'

And they dragged the waiter away.

I'd already shot them down twenty times over, my finger pulling an invisible trigger, before venturing to make my first real movement, which was to put my glass down.

Gradually the sounds of ordinary life came back. I tried to interpret people's expressions. Hatred. Indifference. Horror. Satisfaction. Pain. Compassion.

Monsieur Legendre clenched his fist. I pushed the carafe of water over to him.

'Drink that. You'll feel better.'

Automatically, he drank.

'You see, Monsieur Legendre, there are times when it could be worth while not to take care of my hands – to be actually doing something rather than preparing to be a great pianist.'

I saw him go red. He was feeling awkward.

'This isn't the time,' he stammered. 'Not yet.'

He paid the bill and left the table, inviting me to follow him. Out in the street, he whispered, 'You mustn't assume all those people are cowards, but what can you do in the face of *that*?'

Stopping outside German HQ, he jerked his chin at the two machine guns ready to spit fire and the sandbags piled up in case of siege. Four lorries stood inside the gateway. Soldiers were loading them up.

'Come on, David. Don't stand there.'

It was good to hear him call me David.

'They don't know whether to run for it or sit tight. All they hold now is the town itself. It's the same at militia headquarters – the Maquis are everywhere. We only have to wait a little longer.'

'No, we don't. We mustn't wait. They'll destroy everything as they leave. They've got to be stopped.'

'By you? David against Goliath?'

Maybe he thought he was being funny.

'Yes, by me.'

And I got on my bicycle without saying goodbye, and set off along the road to Brive.

There was no need for Monsieur Legendre to worry. No one was going to reproach him for waiting too long. Another few months and he'd have his little group of pupils back, good little girls and boys coming to play their scales in his flat. He'd give a poor but gifted boy lessons too, out of charity. Music mattered more than anything. But he must close the windows and shutters fast if he heard a burst of machine-gun fire. It's a deafening noise, and gunfire makes poor counterpoint to Mozart. He just had to wait. Poor old Monsieur Legendre!

Well, poor old David, too, wanting to kill the

whole world. As I cycled down the slope from the town walls I felt angry with myself for aiming at the wrong targets. First Monsieur Rigal, then Monsieur Legendre, the only two people who'd really helped me. But they would keep on saying 'Wait'. When you're fifteen you don't want to wait. I pedalled hard downhill. The warm wind dried my tears.

Brive, Paris, my parents. The map of France pinned to the classroom wall in the empty house came back into my mind. I'd looked at it so often, tracing all the stages on the journey that would take me home one day. Right, so that day had come. I had money in my pocket. I'd get on the first train.

But I was so tired and hungry that I had to stop for a rest at the roadside. I sat on a sloping bank in the shade of a hazelnut hedge to get my breath back.

I opened my bag, looking for something to eat. I knew there wasn't anything, but still. So I fed on dreams, stuffed myself with plans. And for want of any alternative I got drunk on Apollinaire's book of poems *Alcools*, sitting there all by myself right in the middle of the war. That book was especially precious; Claire had given it to me.

A cart, a car or a bicycle came along the road now and then and distracted me as I read. My eyes would follow them for a moment, and then I went on reading poetry aloud.

I have had the courage to look behind me
The corpses of my days
Mark my way and I mourn them

Some rot in Italian churches
Or the little lemon groves
Which bear both fruit and flowers
At once and in every season . . .

Why couldn't I get that particular poem out of my head?

The corpses of my days
Mark my way and I mourn them

I wasn't mourning so much as shouting.

'Can't you shut your great gob?'

A voice from nowhere – and certainly not one I recognized – made me jump. A voice which I traced upwards from an old pair of clodhoppers, past a dirty pair of trousers and a checked shirt, to the face of a pimply red-headed youth who was pointing a pistol at me.

I put down Apollinaire, leaning up on one elbow.

'Only if I want to. Anyway it's not a great gob, it's my mouth and it's telling you to push off.'

I started reading again, but a kick in the shin made me look back at the redhead. His face was turning a deeper scarlet all the time, and his pistol was still aimed at me.

School playground stuff, there in the middle of the countryside.

'You don't think I'm scared of you, do you?'

This was true. I was no more scared of the redhead than of some little first-form boy in the playground of the Voltaire Grammar School. The more I looked at him, the redder in the face he went.

'Come on, explain yourself. You tell me to shut up: right, I shut up. So why should it bother you if I carry on reading? You own this place, do you?'

The redhead was trying to look tough, like a prewar film star, and gritting his teeth, which made talking difficult. However, the gist of his remarks, so far as I could gather, was, 'You'd better get moving', along with 'little git' or 'little idiot' – little something or other, anyway. But when the little something or other stood up, I turned out to be as tall as he was. Even though he jammed the pistol into my chest, I could feel him trembling. He was two or three years older than me, with a face scarred by acne.

I pushed his gun aside and asked again, 'What's it to you if I sit in the shade and read a book? If you're after my clothes, help yourself. My bag's over there. But my money's in my pocket.'

I saw him tap his foot: a grubby kid in a temper.

'You mean you think *we're* thieves?'

'Who's *you*?'

He started yelling in the direction of the wood on the other side of the road.

'Here, Thumper, come and lend a hand! He doesn't understand at all.'

This was the first sensible thing I'd heard him say. It was also the first time I'd felt like laughing in a very long while.

I saw Thumper emerge from the bushes, jump the bank and come up to stand beside the redhead. First a pistol, now a shotgun, and both trained on one harmless reader of Apollinaire.

With Thumper at his side, Ginger had recovered his nerve. I felt the fight go out of me. I really didn't mind what they did.

Without a word, Thumper thrust my bag into my arms, grabbed my collar and made me run over the road and into the wood. Ginger followed with my bike over his shoulder.

I was exhausted. Thumper let go of me. He made me walk in front of him, switching me with a stick now and then to drive me on into the forest where the ground was soft underfoot, and laughing.

'Taking a rest on the grass, eh? You and your Apollinaire!'

Thumper was suddenly a person to be reckoned with. 'How do you know what I was reading?' I gasped, out of breath.

He shrugged his shoulders. 'Keep moving, and try not to trip up. We can discuss Apollinaire later.'

Even more surprising, he began reciting verse himself as we went along –

> The sky is starlit with the German shells
> The forest of wonders where I see them dance
> The gun's tune in semiquavers rises and swells –

until the moment when he collapsed on the ground, bringing me with him, while Ginger carried on with his cross-country cycling efforts until he reached us and collapsed as well.

It was impossible to speak. Midges hovered in the

air. All I could do was get my breath back and examine my two kidnappers. The redhead was as scarlet in the face as a beefsteak. Thumper had put his gun down and was inspecting me with a smile. I rather liked the look of Thumper. He wore round glasses and a pair of trousers he must have borrowed from his little brother. He looked quite old, maybe twenty, with several days' growth of beard. Waving his arms about, he tried to chase the midges away. He kept looking at me, with a pleasant smile.

'So you're the sort of character who'll carry on reading with a pistol at your head? Are you brave or are you just stupid?'

I returned his smile.

'Neither. I don't like being ordered about, that's all.'

'Even to save your skin?'

I didn't get that. Ginger interrupted. He was a native of the area; I could tell by his accent.

'You two ought to get on well. You're from Paris, right?' he asked me.

I nodded.

'What do you mean about saving my skin?'

'Look.'

I looked around for whatever might have escaped my notice in our frantic race up over the soft forest floor and the brambles. Thumper and Ginger were kneeling. Finger to his lips, Thumper warned me to keep silent. Then I saw what I should have seen before. The hazelnut hedge under which I'd been sitting and the grass, already withering, at the corner of the road were visible through a gap between the trees. But that wasn't it. A few metres from the bank, spread out in a semi-circle and hidden behind fir trees and bushes, their weapons trained on my little patch of grass, I saw ten Gingers and Thumpers on watch with their backs to us.

I turned to Thumper. His smile had vanished. OK, I got the idea.

Far off, I heard the sound of an engine in the quiet summer air. The solid, prosperous-looking estate car arrived on the right spot at the right minute and the right second. Three grenades were thrown. There was a burst of Sten gun fire. Two Gingers or Thumpers ran down to the road, looking at the burning vehicle, picked up several weapons and came back to us. That was all. It was over.

The little troop prepared to move off. The faces coming towards me were wreathed in smiles. The man who must be leader of the party pointed to me and made a sign to Thumper. Thumper gave the thumbs-up sign and nodded. Then he tapped me on the shoulder.

'The introductions can wait. Come on, we're off. Don't forget the bike, Ginger.'

I picked up my bag and ran down the other side of the hill with them, leaving the burnt-out car behind me.

'And five militiamen fewer! Five!'

I forget which of them was exulting over this macabre piece of arithmetic. I don't know why, but I took a dislike to him. Yet I knew he was right. I'd seen the militia in action. Still, a man's life isn't really a laughing matter. I remembered Lonia's long speeches as she tried to defuse my hatred.

'Life is the most sacred thing there is, children,' she used to say. 'Stronger even than war. Do you understand that?'

Well, of course we did. Everything Lonia said had to be true. And in the end, when all the horrors were over, we'd see our parents again.

Would I ever see Lonia again, though, and all the children the Nazis had taken away early that morning? Life – perhaps *they*, the Nazis, didn't even know the meaning of the word.

As I plunged into the forest with the little troop, Thumper ahead of me pointing out the tree roots in our way, I began to feel doubts. Yes, 'five fewer'. Supposing it had been six, it would have been even better. An eye for an eye. I wanted to hurt them the way they'd hurt me, me and a lot of other people.

I couldn't go along with Lonia's compassion any more. She had lied too. To *them*, the life of a man or a woman or a child was worth nothing. Nothing at all. I hoped they'd die in torment. Perhaps there was a militiaman back there behind us doing just that, still howling. Good. Good. Good.

I had begun to march in step with the others. My boots were crushing the skulls of Nazis, Germans, militiamen, collaborators. I hadn't enough strength in me to take all the revenge I wanted. I'd have liked to hammer the ground even more fiercely, getting my own back on the policemen who came knocking at our door to take my parents away from me.

I was all concentrated hatred as I went along the road leading I didn't know where. I followed the others, envying them the weapons they carried. Let them just give me one, and then I'd show them! Even with the oldest and rustiest of their guns. But all they gave me was the chance to think about the murdered people I'd loved, and a drink of water at the first halt.

I was the odd one out in this company of young men who played real war games. Ill at ease, I crossed and uncrossed my legs, shifting around on the pine needles until Thumper came to my rescue.

'Meet Popol, everyone.'

And all of them, with their Maquis nicknames – Ginger, d'Artagnan, the Professor, Marat and the rest – raised their hands in greeting.

'Why Popol?' I asked Thumper under my breath.

'From Apollinaire, right? You don't want to forget old friends, do you?'

I was grateful to Thumper for making me smile again, in spite of the blisters I had after our forced march to their camp.

I heard the first lookout's whistle. I saw the first huts, men making the evening meal, camouflaged bicycles, the Maquis's two motorbikes.

A few brief words were exchanged; then Thumper introduced me to the captain. He was like the others, perhaps a bit older, and wore a cap in spite of the heat. He gave me an odd look.

'Recruiting babes in arms, Thumper?'

I'd never felt so ashamed in my life. Not even in the showers at the Jesuit boarding school when I used to go into contortions trying to hide my circumcision.

Thumper just shrugged his shoulders.

The captain looked me straight in the eye.

'You a Communist?'

'Why?'

'Never mind why. I ask the questions, you answer them, period.'

'No, I'm a Jew.'

I had no idea what I'd said to make it so hard for the captain and Thumper to restrain their mirth. Did they think being a Jew was so funny?

Trying to keep a straight face, the captain told me to go and wait outside. I had to obey, though I'd have liked to punch his nose first. What could they be saying to each other?

Around me, the others went on with their work, sawing wood, oiling guns. I stood there like an idiot, waiting.

After a bit I'd had enough. I went back into the hut, which was made of branches, prepared to knock the whole place down and holding out my identity card. Thumper and the captain, who were sitting on the camp bed, jumped to their feet.

I waved my card in the air, showing them I was about to tear it up. As if the captain guessed my intention, he grabbed my forearm, squeezing it with all his might until my hand was forced to drop the miserable scrap of paper.

'Don't be silly, David Grunbaum! We can still use false identity cards.'

David Grunbaum. He'd actually said, 'David Grunbaum'. My name.

Their faces looked different now. So they knew about me?

My anger melted away as I heard my name spoken, my real name, all of it, for the first time in two years. My throat hurt. My eyes pricked. I was going to burst into tears. No, I wasn't. I managed to hold the tears back, looking away. Thanks, Thumper. Thanks, captain. How could I convey my gratitude, standing there like a fool? My name. My parents' name. And then the tears came after all.

They gave me as much time as I needed. Then Thumper took my hand and led me out into the open air.

I shall never forget Thumper, his glasses all misted up. He took me round the camp. A dozen young men were learning how to handle a new weapon. I heard the word 'American', but I wasn't particularly interested. Thumper knew very well what I wanted to ask him, and *I* knew he was taking me off somewhere private so I could let the question burst out of me.

'How did you know? I mean, it's not written all over my face!'

Thumper gazed into the distance, very far away, towards other thickly wooded valleys.

'We know everything in the Maquis.'

'Oh, come off it!'

He looked sad. 'Well, we knew that only one boy had escaped the raid. We knew his name. And when I saw your bicycle plate with the village number on it, we simply put two and two together. I was right, wasn't I?'

He told me how he'd worked it out, not at all boastfully, almost pityingly, holding my hand quite tightly in his.

But I'd had enough of that kind of thing! Wasn't I ever going to be like other people? I could see it in Thumper's face: the same expression I'd seen in the faces of Monsieur Rigal and Monsieur Legendre. All I needed was a 'poor child' or so, just to emphasize my wretchedness. So far as other people were concerned I'd always be the Jew, or the sole survivor, or the Jew who'd been the sole survivor. They'd work it all out: my story, my unhappiness, everything I'd suffered. But those were *my* experiences. And now I wanted to be rid of them.

Thumper's sympathy got me down. I already knew everything he could say off by heart. I could have dictated his next speech to him. It was coming any moment now, serious, emotional, full of horrible kindness. I wished to God they'd leave me in peace! I didn't want to be made to feel it all twice over! The hell with their compassion!

I tried to pull my hand away from Thumper's and couldn't. Lost in thought, he had no idea of his own strength. I waited. And none of what I was expecting happened.

Thumper let go of my hand. He cleared his throat.

'Listen, David. Until G. has been liberated you'd better stick to the identity you had. You're not Jewish. You're known as Popol: that's just a straightforward matter of security. Not a word of your own story to anyone at all. You can make up any tale you like – I leave it to you. Otherwise, you're under my command.'

If there hadn't been anyone around to see us I'd have hugged him.

'Then I can kill Germans too!'

Thumper said all in good time, and they'd squeeze up a bit in his hut to make room for me.

So now I was one of them. A member of the Maquis. Going by the name of Popol and ready to fight. I smoked my first cigarette; I don't think I'll go into that here. Possibly it was what they call a baptism of fire. I could have devoured Germans all day, but all I actually got to eat in the evening was a wretched little canned sardine with potatoes, boiled or mashed or baked in the ashes of the fire. I learned to shave, sing, assemble an automatic pistol and take it apart again. I filched a couple of chickens from nearby farms by night. I grumbled about the inaccuracy of the parachute drops. My moment of glory came when I translated the English instructions for using the Gammon grenades which did get through. I got accustomed to the life, ready to strike camp the moment the alarm was given.

I became lookout man, cook, brilliant strategist bending over a staff officer's map. I juggled with the forces opposing the Nazis: the partisans, the French Forces of the Interior, the Communists, the Gaullists. For two pins I'd have blown up a train and diverted a whole brigade of Germans single-handed. I'd have outdone the Brave Little Tailor of my father's bedtime stories.

Thumper kept an eye on me. Sometimes he took me off on our own, and I turned back into the adolescent of fifteen I really still was all the time. With him, listening to his voice, which was always equable and never reproachful, I silently apologized to him for all my grand play-acting, but he never mentioned it.

Sitting beside me in the warmth of the evening, with all the fires out as a precaution, he would look at the sky, the stars, the clouds sailing by. His voice was grave. He was always talking about the future, a future that was coming closer and closer now, and everything he was going to do then. Go back to his studies, see his parents again, train to be a teacher. So far as he was concerned killing Germans was no fun.

'If we have to kill them, it's only to make them go away and leave us in peace. I don't care about anything else. Anyone who likes can have my gun. War is horrible. But I'll see it through to the end; you bet I will. It can't be much longer now.'

And he ran his hand over my mop of hair.

I liked hearing him talk about his own escape. He'd run away to join the Maquis and avoid being sent to do forced labour in Germany. He told me what it was like in the Maquis at first: no weapons, nothing, begging from farm to farm, and always afraid of being denounced, arrested and tortured.

'It's different now. The Allies have landed and the Germans are on the run. G. will be taken in a couple of weeks. The town's surrounded by the Maquis.'

'And then what?'

'Then I'm going straight into the library and I'm going to pinch the first novel I lay my hands on. Two years without reading a line – think of that!'

I could hardly imagine it. And there was such sadness in his voice. I left him alone with the moon and the stars, went to our hut, and came back at once carrying my copy of *Alcools*, which I'd sworn to keep all my life. I put it on his lap.

Thumper pressed my shoulder with one hand, took off his glasses and wiped his eyes.

I was sorry I'd made him cry, but I owed it to him. His voice talking in the evening reminded me of the bedtime stories Mother and Father used to tell me as a child. 'Have a good night, see you in the morning,' they'd say. And I did have a good night, lulled to sleep.

I never told Thumper about that, but I was aware of it all right. He calmed my savage feelings and gave me a glimpse of a future when life would go on. He sometimes made me laugh, a real laugh which swept everything else away.

I wonder if he still remembers our expedition to get food supplies?

'Come on, Popol, wake up. We're off.'

'Where to?'

'Wait and see.'

This was my first real expedition with the Maquis. They trusted me! Thumper gave me a pistol and ammunition.

'Your gun, Popol.' And he added, very gravely, 'Don't let it fall into enemy hands, whatever you do.'

The column set off. Five of us for whatever our mission was. An ambush? In any event we went all the way down to the village. I brought up the rear. It was one of the most important positions, although I got a crick in the neck from glancing back, pistol in hand.

I couldn't make out what the other four were up to. Lanky was whistling, Ginger was singing, Castanets was looking at the ground, his sub-machine-gun casually tied to his back with string, and Thumper walked in front with his own gun over his shoulder. Obviously they were relying on me to protect them.

I got my surprise when we reached the village. Instead of keeping in the shelter of the walls, Thumper marched straight down the middle of the road. I was walking backwards to give them cover until we reached the village hall. No 'Hands up'. No terrified faces. Only the village mayor coming to meet Thumper, looking annoyed.

'Oh, hell, Thumper, couldn't you have picked some other place? You've been coming here for the last two months. OK, OK, I'll give you your coupons. All the same, don't you know any other villages?'

Thumper winked at me.

The mayor produced ration cards from his safe. Thumper took a requisitioning draft out of his pocket, to be reimbursed after the Liberation. They shook hands, and we turned round.

Leaving the village, I asked, 'Is that all?'

Thumper looked at me.

'What did you think we were going to do? Attack a coachload of Germans?'

'So I wasn't any real use at all?'

'Yes, you were, Popol, you kept us company. If you hadn't come along you'd have had a very boring morning.'

I'd have hit him if Lanky hadn't burst out laughing. It was infectious. My fury dissolved into laughter too. I laughed so much it hurt.

'A raid like that is good for a medal any day,' Ginger assured me.

'You rats, you were having me on!'

They picked me up by my arms and legs and carried me back to camp. After a bit I stopped struggling. I had porters to carry me; I could lie and get tanned in the sun. This was the life!

'You won't fool me another time,' I promised them.

Thumper bent down to me.

'There won't be another time.'

'Why not? Don't you trust me any more?'

'No, it's not that. Next time will be for real.'

I stopped laughing. But I wish Thumper could have known how good he made me feel, laughing and looking up at the sun as my porters swung me back and forth. Two months of misery, anger, indifference, despair, smiles, hatred, and suddenly the whole thing broke up in laughter.

And then the day came.

No one in camp was shooting his mouth off now. Orders were given briefly.

'Any questions?'

I did have a question, but I held my tongue. Suppose I died, who would tell my parents? I guessed there were similar questions in my friends' heads as they tried to smile. Smiles of fear worn like a handsome row of decorations. We wanted to get on and get it over with.

Our target was the German HQ. Twenty or so of the garrison had barricaded themselves in. The idea was to take the place, but spare civilians.

A saying of my father's came back to me as I observed our preparations for departure. 'You've got pins in the behind!' It was a literal translation from Yiddish, and he used to say it to me when I couldn't keep still. I could hear the irritation in his voice as I watched my comrades, assembling their weapons, taking them apart, oiling them for the last time, going off to pee for the last time but one, combing their hair, straightening scarves or armbands. Any activity to escape the fear lurking deep down – but there was joy too. Only a few hours to go until the Liberation. The end of the nightmare.

I didn't leave Thumper's side. I was so jittery I even felt bold enough to ask, 'Can I stay with you, Thumper?'

His face looked gaunt, and he kept readjusting his glasses. He nodded.

'No fooling about, though, Popol! In a few hours' time you'll be David Grunbaum again, for good.'

How did he always know what to say? My fear vanished. I wasn't going to liberate the town of G., I was going to liberate my own name. That was the best thing of all. I might come to appreciate other things, but only later. I was relieved, but afraid for Thumper at the same time. I hoped he'd be all right. Well, of course he would, because I was going to be beside him. I'd be his lucky mascot. I was magic.

As we watched the long column get under way in the dust of August, Thumper dug his elbow into my ribs. He whispered a line of verse:

A very fine thing is war

And we couldn't help laughing. Apollinaire was with us!

One of the lads I didn't know so well turned round. 'You poor bloody idiots! As if this was any kind of fun. You need a couple of bullets in you, that'd show you.'

I looked suitably crestfallen, and Thumper copied me, but we were still laughing inside.

Just before reaching G. we joined forces with another column as strong as our own now was. Six hundred men against twenty or so Germans. They hadn't a chance.

We carried out our orders to the letter. We were to surround the town: ten scouts and an attack party for every route into G.

I was ready for anything: the sound of shooting, bursts of sub-machine-gun fire. I met with total, terrifying silence, closed shutters, and as we approached their HQ the surprising sight of a pitiful group of elderly Germans, with a white flag ahead of them and their hands in the air. G. had been taken.

Suddenly there was a tremendous noise all over the town. Shutters were flung open, flags waved, there was applause, shouts of *'Vive la France!'* and people bellowing the Marseillaise at the top of their voices. Joy broke out, almost more terrifying than fear, in the ringing of bells and the sounding of sirens, in embraces and tears and shouts.

The more responsible part of the column marched on to the Town Hall, although the string holding Lanky's Bren gun in place had broken.

I walked beside Thumper, proud, my chest thrust out, no jacket on. Any of us who says he didn't weep for joy that day is lying. I wept for sadness too, looking for Claire in the crowd and failing to find her.

She wasn't at her house either. I went to look the moment we got permission to break ranks. Then I wandered round the walls, lost in the town I knew so well, taking no notice of the surrender of collaborators pointed out by people who'd been resistance workers for the last few seconds and wanted them punished then and there. I heard several shots fired, then a shout of: 'Popol! The Maquis secretary wants you. He's been looking for you everywhere.'

It was Thumper.

'He can come and find me, then.'

'Don't be an idiot. He sent me.'

Thumper's face, wreathed in smiles; then the reserved face of a man I didn't know, seated at a large desk in the Town Hall.

'Given up saluting, have you?'

I looked at him in annoyance. 'Stand to attention!' he shouted.

I still didn't move. I stood there with my hands in my pockets.

'Here, you pig-headed boy.'

He stood up, came round in front of the desk and handed me a piece of paper. I accepted it disdainfully. Thumper raised his voice for the first time.

'Look at it, you idiot!'

I looked at it. It was me in the photograph, and my name on the brand-new identity card I'd been handed. Grunbaum, David, born on . . . at . . .

I quickly put my hand to my back pocket.

'You won't find the old one there. I pinched it last night,' Thumper told me.

I flung myself at the stern-faced man, almost

knocking him over in my delight. He hugged me for what seemed like ages. Then I stepped back, saluted impeccably, and raced away.

Sitting in the bright sunlight on the steps outside the Town Hall, I looked at my name, written in fine calligraphy. My own name. A present from Thumper, who came up and took my shoulder.

'Here, you have to sign it. It's not valid without your signature.'

He handed me a fountain pen. I put the identity card on a step, knelt down and signed it. Imitating my father's handwriting in my signature, the way I used to copy it in my rough notebook at school. Kneeling there, I held back my tears, and Thumper didn't notice anything. I even managed a joke as I returned his pen.

'Did you think that was so urgent, just now? I thought you were going straight to the library to pinch a book.'

He smiled at me. 'Come on. We'd better get some sleep. We're on guard tonight.'

He took me off to the school where, two months earlier, I'd sometimes trembled over a misplaced participle. Thumper guessed nothing of my feelings at the sight of the headmaster's office, the main courtyard and the classrooms.

Only two months before, I'd been hiding out in the home for Jewish children. But officially I wasn't Jewish, my friends and parents were missing, and I went to that school to study so that I could make something of myself later on. Well, 'later on' was now. David Grunbaum, aged fifteen, a pistol in his belt, lying down to sleep in the covered part of the requisitioned school courtyard.

The camp beds weren't even up before Thumper fell asleep. I couldn't sleep myself. I just lay there thinking of my luck, if that was the word. Of being alive. I was alive.

The empty house was not so very far away. I remembered my first night there.

A yell. Maurice fighting an invisible enemy in his bed.

'No, no! You'll never catch me. No! The Germans, the Germans, they're coming to kill us . . . Mummy! Mummy!'

Maurice flailed about him in the air. 'Take that, and that, and that!'

His cries didn't rouse anyone. I got up, went over to him, took him by the shoulders and shook him.

'Maurice. Wake up, Maurice. It's me, David. You're going to be all right. Hey, look at me.'

He went on struggling.

'They mustn't, they mustn't!'

I shook him even harder.

'Stop it, for goodness' sake! You're having a nightmare, that's all. There, it's over now, see? Are you listening?'

Slowly, Maurice stopped threshing about. He was sweating. I wiped his forehead and his face with a corner of the sheet.

'Honestly, it's over. There – now you can go to sleep again.'

'Suppose it comes back?'

'I'm here with you. Anyway, it won't come back.'

'Oh yes, it will. It's like this every night.'

I made Maurice lie down again, tucked him in, and went back to my own bed. 'Here, give me your hand, Maurice. The nightmare's gone for good now, you see if it hasn't.'

Maurice reached out his arm, took my hand and went to sleep.

The empty house was only a few minutes' bicycle ride away. I remembered my first morning there.

Little Perla, aged five, walking in the garden with me. Woods far away in the distance.

'Lonia said I was to show you everything and not leave anything out,' she told me. 'Look, that's where I hide when we play hide-and-seek.'

She pointed to the trunk of a big tree. I smiled, looking down at her serious expression and her pigtails.

'But they always find me,' she added, and then went on without any change of tone, 'Where do you come from? How did you get away? Where are your parents? Were they tortured?'

I picked Perla up and hugged her tight. She went on whispering in my ear. 'Hey, did you see my mummy where you've come from?'

I hugged her even harder to make her shut up, and then put her down again. I forced myself to laugh.

'First to reach the tree has won!'

Perla touched the tree first, happy and breathless. She pointed to two children digging the garden near the steps leading up to the house.

'That's Maurice and Hanna. They're in love. Come on, I'll show you.'

Hanna and Maurice weren't getting on very well; their spades were too big for them. They were perspiring and muddy. Seeing me coming, Maurice looked serious. 'We have to finish two more rows,' he said. 'It's in our interests, after all. We wouldn't have enough to eat without the vegetable garden.'

Hanna wasn't so brave. 'Maybe, but I'm stopping now.'

She drove her spade into the soil, but not hard enough. It fell over. Hanna went to sit on the bottom step. Maurice abandoned his work too, and the pair of them sat side by side, their legs touching. Perla was gleeful.

'See! Told you so! Told you they were in love.'

Maurice looked at her crossly. I sat down on the ground to ask some questions. 'Have you all been here long?'

'I came first,' said Hanna. 'Maurice and Perla came soon afterwards, but I'm different, you see. My parents sent me here to hide me. So all right, maybe they don't write, but that's just to protect me. They'll be here the moment the war's over.'

Perla jumped up. 'Liar! You *are* just the same as us, so there! You don't know where your parents are. I'm going to tell Lonia you tell lies.'

'You dare!'

I asked Maurice about himself.

'My parents were fired on, just as we were crossing the demarcation line into the free zone. They died. I managed to escape. That's all there is to it. Come on, Hanna, we have to get this finished.'

I shook my head, shaking off a bad dream. Perla took my hand.

'Don't worry, they're all like that. Listen, did you really see my mummy where you've come from?'

I remembered what they said, what I said, their gestures, my gestures. How could I fall asleep, even with Thumper to protect me? Where were Perla and Hanna now? Where were their parents? Where were mine?

I suddenly got up. I needed air. All these questions, locked away too long by my hope of the Liberation, liberating themselves now unasked. My place wasn't here any longer. I felt quite sure of that out in the streets of a town given up to rejoicing, busy restoring requisitioned cars and food supplies to their owners.

Worst of all was seeing my former Maquis comrades outside their own front doors, with their parents beside them. They were handing in their weapons. It was not at all nice of me. Even under torture I wouldn't have admitted to my jealousy, but that's what it was: my sick feeling and sense of anticlimax, my wild desire to be like them.

I hurried back to the school and woke Thumper.

'What is it?'

'Nothing. Look, I'm off. I just came to say goodbye.'

'Oh, let me sleep, will you? There's still work to do.'

He turned over.

I sat down on his bed. 'OK, Thumper, if you don't want to listen I'll just say goodbye, and thanks for everything.'

He was already fast asleep again. I kissed his forehead.

Paris on the horizon, and all my illusions. I didn't have much to carry. I could get on the first train and life would open out ahead of me. I wanted to find my mother and father, and what a marvellous celebration we'd have then! They were all I had. No uncles, aunts, brothers, sisters, cousins or grandparents. Only my parents, to hug, to talk to, and I'd talk my fill, making up for two years of unbearable silence. Or I might say nothing, simply look at them. Looks are just as eloquent as words. I carried their photograph with me, and I could read so much in their eyes. I wanted to fling myself into their arms, feel the warmth of their bodies. Surely I'd find my mother and father at last at the end of the road!

The train idea didn't work: all the railway lines had been sabotaged. That couldn't be helped; nor could I have known. It wasn't by my own choice I'd ended up in a children's home so close to the fighting at the time of the liberation of Brive. I saw the enemy surrender on 15 August. I heard about the Allied landing in Provence. I heard tales of horror and famine. I stored up thousands of pictures as dreadful as those my father's friend Yantel remembered from the time when they'd emigrated from Poland. None of that mattered too much. France was free and I was going to find my parents. Nothing counted except the days still separating us.

I used any means of transport that came my way. I forced a motorist to give me a lift back in the direction of my parents. Only the minutes counted now. Soon it would be just a matter of seconds, after over a month of frantic travelling.

Paris. The end of my nightmare.

I got out of the Simca, with an apologetic gesture to the driver. He understood. He was a kindly old pensioner on his way to join his own family.

Paris was liberated. So the news I'd heard on the way was really true. I'd be home in . . . well, time didn't matter any more. I was sure my parents would be waiting for me, so why hurry? I could wander through the streets before going down into the Métro, smelling the electric, indefinable smell of the underground railway.

There was an after-the-party feel about Paris. I saw the remains of barricades, French Forces of the Interior men on patrol, some of the German signposts burnt, others still being torn up. There were tricolour flags at the windows, garlands waving in the wind, faded flowers lying in the road.

A city full of women, children and old people. I walked slowly. I saw burnt-out cars, German tanks abandoned at crossroads, torn posters, walls daubed with paint. It was a lovely summer evening when I reached the République underground station. I wanted Line 9.

I attracted some funny looks in the carriage, and realized I'd better conceal my gun under my shirt. The old Dubonnnet advertisements I'd known since childhood were still there. Everything was the way it used to be. Except that I caught sight of a different David in shop windows, one I hadn't taken the time to inspect properly. He looked dirty, shaggy and ill-shaven.

I ran a hand through my greasy hair. I suddenly felt uneasy as I got off the train at Porte de Montreuil. I wiped my damp hands on the dungarees I'd stolen five hundred kilometres away. My palms were still sticky, and I walked unsteadily. I was sweating as I reached the Rue de Paris. Nothing had changed here. At the corner of the Rue Robespierre, I waved to Madame Latour. She waved back without really knowing who I was. In the Rue Marceau I saw paving stones torn up to build a barricade, but there were chairs out on the pavement, and people were chatting to each other. I turned left. My own street. My own block of flats was just after the red brick wall.

I'd been running a mad race, certain I'd find the people I loved, clinging to hope in spite of everything and everyone. And I'd won. My revenge. My triumph, as I knocked with all my might.

The door opened. Mother wasn't there. A figure in a nightdress looked at me in mingled alarm, curiosity and distaste, and then slammed the door in my face.

Perhaps I was on the wrong floor. No, the damp patch on the wall beside the door frame that used to annoy Father so much was still there. The corridor light worked by the time switch had gone off. I located the switch again without even having to look, so this really was my front door and my flat all right. I began knocking again, kicking as well this time.

There was a bellow on the other side of the door, and it opened abruptly.

My hall inside.

'Stop pestering us, will you, you little bastard? I'll teach you to go knocking people up at this time of day! I've got to go to work tomorrow. What do you want?'

Around fifty, in underpants and vest, obviously the local tough guy. Next moment he'd grabbed me by the shirt, ready to fling me back out on the landing.

A declaration of war. I'd trained my pistol on him. Watching me, speechless and stunned, he retreated to the dining room. One word out of him and I'd shoot. He was scared enough to be careful. His wife had now turned up and was standing beside him.

I saw things in there I'd rather not have seen. Instead of my piano, a hideous Henri II-style sideboard. Instead of the sewing machine, an armchair covered in flock velour. Instead of – but there was no point in listing what wasn't there. I opened the bedroom door.

They'd been sleeping in my parents' sheets, in their bed.

I bit my lip until the blood came to stop myself shooting this revolting couple who'd left their slimy traces on everything. I made them sit down.

I had my breath back now.

'What have you done with my piano?'

The man was stammering. 'We sold it. We sold almost everything. We didn't know, did we? They gave us permission to have the flat, but look, you can take what you like. There's a little money – you can have that too.'

I sat down, placing the pistol in front of me, my mind vacant. Should I shoot them? I shrugged my shoulders as I looked at the miserable pair in front of me. Should I frighten them? They were already terrified, offering to make things up to me. There was no way they could do that.

I rose to my feet, cast a desultory glance around my own bedroom, and closed the door again.

'What about papers and photographs? What have you done with them?'

The answer was muttered. 'Threw the lot away. They told us you'd never be b . . . '

He stopped. I cocked the pistol. My voice was

expressionless. 'Right. You can go. Go on, just as you are.'

They looked at me imploringly.

'I'll count to three.'

I watched them scurry into the hall in nightdress and underwear. The door slammed. I pressed the trigger and fired a single shot.

If only I'd fired at myself, I wouldn't have had to spend the night alone in our empty flat, searching for a past that had crumbled away, opening wardrobes to find Father's made-over suits and Mother's dresses inside.

I wanted to die. It was the first time I'd really wanted to die. But there was still a tiny gleam of hope. Mother and Father might come back later.

I sat down on the bed. I'd wait for ever, if need be. No, that was ridiculous.

I took my revenge. I emptied the wardrobe, tore the sheets, kicked china about, wrecked the kitchen, doing it all quite coldly, while all the time I was howling and hurting and weeping inside.

I went back to my own bedroom, which was being used as a lumber room. I smiled. They hadn't touched my *Count of Monte Cristo*. I picked it up and sniffed it. All my unhappiness ebbed away. I read, as I used to read in the days when Mother and Father were still there, and I was helping Edmond Dantès to escape – 'And put the light out now, David, you'll harm your eyes reading so late. Sleep, *Kindele*, sleep, my little one.' I felt really happy.

Small, precise knocks at the door. I jumped,

picked up my pistol, and went to open it.

When I saw who it was I could hardly believe it. I flung my arms round her and hugged her hard enough to suffocate her and stop her crying. I felt her nails dig into my back. Madame Bianchotti. I owed her my life: she'd hidden me on the morning of the big raid. I found I could cry at last.

'Come along, David.'

She took my hand and we sat down in the dining room, looking at each other in silence. Her eyes were shining with mingled happiness and sadness. I don't know what she saw in mine.

'I prayed for you every day, David, you and your parents, and God heard me.'

I forgave her for her God, her lighted candles, her prayers. She disarmed my hatred.

I don't know how long we sat there saying nothing, hand in hand, until words came back to us at last, silly words.

How I'd changed – oh goodness, how I'd grown! I mustn't be in a hurry. I had plenty of time to tell her everything. She was so happy! My parents – well, I must be patient. The war wasn't over yet. The prisoners would be coming back a bit later, when Germany had surrendered. And then I'd get my flat and the shop back, and everything would be the same as before.

I didn't have time to explain that nothing could be the same as before, because of Lonia, Maurice, Hanna, the twins, little Perla, Ida, Rachel, Samuel, Hélène . . . no, she couldn't understand. Perhaps they would all be going home too.

The bell rang. There was a violent knocking. Madame Bianchotti knew who it was, and so did I. We both smiled broadly. I walked nonchalantly to the door and opened it.

Monsieur and Madame Whatsitsname stood there, wrapped in blankets and sheltering behind two policemen.

Monsieur Whatsit had recovered his confidence. 'That's him. That's him all right. We're good citizens, we pay our rent, and then this young rascal . . . '

That young rascal had now had time to put on his partisan armband. Pistol in hand, I leaned against the door-frame.

'What is it? This is no time of night to go waking people in their own homes.'

My armband, my pistol, the alarm in the eyes of the policemen, the spluttering noises they were making – yes, I was sure of it.

'You were here two years ago, weren't you? In this very spot, looking for my parents. Didn't have too much trouble finding your way back, I hope?'

'Look – it was orders. We were only carrying out orders.'

'Don't worry, I'm taking my things and leaving.' I looked straight at Monsieur and Madame Whatsitsname. 'But I'll be back. This is my place, so meanwhile don't forget the housework.'

Madame Bianchotti rejoined me. 'Come up to my flat, David.'

Out on the landing an extraordinary thing happened. Tiny little Madame Bianchotti, who always wore a black dress and an aura of religious devotion, spat at the policemen's feet. The spitting image of decency, you might say.

In her flat, I went to the window from which I'd watched my parents leave and seen their eyes for the last time. I was hoping to see them reappear exactly as they looked when they were taken away, carrying suitcases, blankets over their shoulders. My illusion was swiftly shattered. I drew the curtain.

There was a photograph of Monsieur Bianchotti on the mantelpiece.

'He died of grief last year. Over our son, you know.'

I did know. I had been sleeping in their dead son's room for several days before the raid. I'd been very angry with my parents at the time. Murderously angry. I'd sworn at them and insulted them. Jacob and Clara Grunbaum. Today I asked their pardon.

Madame Bianchotti kept close to me.

'God alone holds our lives in his hands. He brought you back.'

I must have grown up a bit, since I didn't made a cutting reply. I went over and hugged her.

'You can stay in Bertrand's room as long as you like.'

I dropped on the bed which had once belonged to

Bertrand, who had 'died for France', and slept under the crucifix on the wall.

Every day brought its own little note of happiness or unhappiness; ding-dong they went, like the sound of the church bells which called Madame Bianchotti to Mass.

On the first morning, washed, shaved and all dressed up in a made-over pair of Bertrand's trousers, I raced downstairs. In passing, I refrained from kicking the door of my flat to scare the two skunks inside. They'd pay later. I wanted to see our shop; that mattered more just now.

Memories hurt when they came up against a rusty iron shutter, still lowered, and a broken window smeared with dust. The enamel sign showed only the BAUM of my name. Tears fell on my white shirt with its rolled-up sleeves.

I got my forehead dirty peering through the window at a shop which used to be full of life. Well, it would be full of life again. I just had to wait and arm myself with patience, or so Madame Bianchotti had assured me. I'd have preferred to use a different kind of weapon. I'd had to hide my pistol, slipping it under a pile of linen in Bertrand's room.

The little notice saying JEWISH FIRM had been torn down. By someone feeling brave at the eleventh hour? I couldn't control my anger: it embraced everyone, including whoever had turned my father's tailor's shop into a ruin. I'd ruin them in their turn if I could, they could count on that.

I should never have come back to Paris. I was sorry now I'd left Thumper, still hunting down Germans and collaborators. They ought all to be killed, executed without trial and without mercy. I'd had enough of my stupid scruples.

I turned back to look at Monsieur Armellino's abandoned cabinet-maker's shop. Some cretin or other had smashed the glazed canopy over the door. Well, he would never be back.

I crossed the road and tried, without much hope, to open the door of his shop. I'd never sit there among the sawdust and shavings again. I'd never hear Monsieur Armellino's voice, promising me that some day everything would be all right.

Everything seemed far from all right as I began making my way round my old haunts for the first time. I couldn't shake off the thought of what Madame Bianchotti had told me about Monsieur Armellino. I'd never see him again. I'd never laugh at his height again; he was only one metre forty-five. I wouldn't hear him reassuring me, telling me that *they* would leave as fast as *they* had come, all of them would leave.

They were leaving all right. But *they* had made him leave first. The Gestapo had come to arrest him one afternoon after someone denounced him. He had defended himself to the last, firing on the rats before killing himself.

Just one short story to add to all the others.

Monsieur Armellino on the ground with a bullet

through his head: a dreadful picture, one I wanted to shake off quickly.

I had already reached the Rue de Paris, and I hadn't really seen anything. I made myself look. Life would still go on without Monsieur Armellino and without my parents. It would go on until I died of it.

Madame Bianchotti had warned me. 'You won't find a lot that's changed.'

She was right. The charcoal dealer's business on the corner was open. As it also sold wines my father used to regard it as a den of vice, but I was glad to go in there today, see the same old transactions over the delivery of ice blocks, meet the same old regulars.

The Kursaal was still there, and the Montreuil Palace. So was the row of shops. The bakery I used to visit. The newsagent. The watchmaker. I stopped outside the display windows for a few minutes to show everyone I was there. But no one took any notice of me. No one, apart from me, took any notice of the other shops, the ones I was really interested in. Their shutters were down. Their proprietors had unpronounceable names. People could get their tongues around Grunbaum, maybe, but how about Flajszakier?

Madame Bianchotti wasn't quite right: something had changed. All the places where I used to wait about, feeling bored, when I went visiting with my father who never tired of talking to the Grinblats, the Nusbaums, the Staroswiekis: those businesses were little black holes among the other shops now.

Hands in pockets, looking casual, I knocked at doors which no one opened, or if anyone did the face was unfamiliar.

'Sorry to bother you. I must be on the wrong floor.'

I went upstairs. I came downstairs, rubbing my eyes at each landing. One more door. One more bell to ring. One more time to turn away without even waiting.

Then, suddenly, I heard the cry of 'David!' I'd hardly hoped for.

'David! David! Is it really you? Come in, *mein Ourem Kind, mein Kindele, mein Chepsele*!'

Madame Treiber hugged me and could hardly bear to let me go. She was crying out loud, laughing and weeping.

'You recognize me, David? You do recognize me?'

I was really grateful to her for abandoning French in favour of a deafening barrage of Yiddish. I hardly minded what she was saying, or the fact that I didn't understand any of it. She was making me a present of my parents' language, music I hadn't heard for months and months. When my father came back, the air of our flat would be full of words like Madame Treiber's, and Mother would reply in the same language. It was the language Lonia used to Samuel when she cuddled him and sang him a lullaby. Perhaps the music of the words gave

Samuel some slight feeling of pleasure, perhaps he found the brightness of past warmth in them. No one would ever know. I thought of him as Madame Treiber held me tight in her arms, and I thought of the music of that language into which I'd been born, which had always surrounded me even if I hadn't taken any notice of it.

I wept. And I felt sorry I hadn't been able to take Samuel in my own arms and whisper words in Yiddish to him, words of which I understood nothing but the sound. Where was Samuel now? Where was Lonia? Where were they all, all the people I'd abandoned?

Eventually Madame Treiber let go of me. Sitting over a cup of black-market tea, she told me about the Jablons, Zylberbergs and Grumbergs, who were all hiding in the country. When the wolf had gone they would come out of hiding again, come home, open up their shops, and 'Everything vill be same like it vos before, David!' Perhaps. Except that I'd never make fun of her accent again.

She looked at me, and began sobbing again. She had no idea what had happened to my parents and all the rest who were taken away that July day. But they'd be back, she told me; she was sure of that. They'd gone to Drancy first, then to a big labour camp. She told me all this in her heavy Yiddish accent, and I wasn't able to keep the promise I'd just made myself. But she was glad to see me smile. 'Her' David was feeling better. She had comforted him. 'Her' David only had to wait for his parents now.

I waited for eight months, eight months which I'd rather not resuscitate in the ordinary light of day. Eight months staying with Madame Bianchotti while I kept an eye on my own flat two floors below.

Months, days, hours, minutes and seconds of hope and despair. I would feel quite calm one day, then full of euphoria or anger the next. I don't like to remember that time. But it still comes back to my memory, just as the Jablons, Zylberbergs and Grumbergs began coming back – particularly after November, when trains were able to cross the river Loire again. A little life returned to our world, although the bread we ate was as coarse as ever. People were coming back. They were coming back, and that meant a tiny gleam of happiness. But their return was painful too, for it left me feeling lonelier than ever. To tell the truth, and though I'm ashamed to admit it, the news of Madame Rosenberg's death gave me a brief moment of nasty, unattractive, ignoble but genuine joy. I wasn't the only person left on my own. And anyway my parents would be coming back. I was lucky, even though I featured as a 'poor child' again, a child to whom people opened their doors wide, very ready to tell me how hard life had been 'down there'. Down there in the country they'd needed false papers, they had to be wary of Germans and denunciations, buy the local people's silence, accept the fact that they must sell their jewels in order to eat.

'You've no idea what it was like, David!'

The hardships they'd suffered 'down there' were – oh, anything they cared to say. I'd stopped listening. I was still suffering hardships of my own, things they wouldn't know about, pleased as they were to get back to their usual games of cards and put their flats in order again. I compared their hardships with mine, but of course all that was nothing beside other hardships suffered in places we only found out about later. When we did we were struck absolutely silent.

Meanwhile, they chattered away and I shrivelled up inside. I could always win any competition in unhappiness. I kept quiet. Their mundane schemes for survival didn't compare with what I'd been through in that remote corner of the Lot valley where the home for Jewish children stood. I resented the fact, and then suddenly felt grateful to them for their interest in me.

'Let's see, how old would you be now, David?'

I resented that too. I might be 'David' again, but there was no room in my memory for my birthday. It was recorded only on my identity card and in the Town Hall register.

By dint of being fifteen years old, however, I eventually got to be sixteen.

I preferred to celebrate my sixteenth birthday alone and in secret, keeping quiet about it, in my bedroom on a cold December day. The newspaper

Le Parisien had announced the reopening of the Paris-to-Brest railway line.

Alone? I wasn't really alone. I felt sure that however far away they were, my parents were with me in their thoughts, anxious about me and happy for me. A birth is always something to be celebrated, even with tears in your eyes. Not that anyone could see mine. Madame Bianchotti was asleep. I placed the bar of chocolate I'd saved for the occasion on the bedspread. In the dim light, I put the candle from my bedside table on the chocolate, making it melt. I started humming, 'Happy Birthday to You', blew out the candle and ate the entire bar of chocolate. Then I lay down and lit a Navy Cut which I smoked slowly, feeling proud of myself and proud of my parents. They would find a son who was older now but who'd never let them down. I thanked them for giving me life. Life was good, even the frugal life of today, in fact better than when birthdays meant lots of presents as in the past. That was the best birthday I'd had.

Madame Bianchotti, however, was not pleased. The brown mark on the bedspread, the ashes on the floor and the sweetish smell of American cigarettes offended against the memory of her son, and her weary look let me know it. It was the same look she'd given me when I took down the crucifix and put the photograph of my parents in the frame meant for Bertrand's picture. She would pray for me. Her piety infuriated me. As if her God forbade her to call a spade a spade, shout at me or shake me.

She was so full of horrible sympathy, with her sighs and her eyes raised to heaven. Not that any more bombs were likely to fall from the heavens now. The Germans might be threatening Strasbourg, but that was a long way off. And anyway, the Allies would have won within a few months, as the radio kept on telling us.

Madame Bianchotti was always turning the other cheek. What was the good of resisting? I moved the bed. I rearranged the room in my own tasteless way. I never aired it and I let everything lie about on the floor. The only result was that I felt uncomfortable, and also sorry for Madame Bianchotti because she felt sorry for me. Like a little black mouse, she would walk for kilometres when she heard any news of a delivery of food or charcoal. Without ever saying a really cross word all through that icy winter she managed to make me feel ashamed.

I realized that fully at breakfast one day, when she had gone out. Sitting down, still sleepy, I automatically picked up the bread and margarine in front of me. As I raised it to my mouth I knew what a fool I'd been. That margarine, part of the fat ration, was on the table every morning only because of the determination of a good little woman whom I was trampling underfoot from the lofty heights of my own unhappiness. Suppose my parents knew!

I could almost feel my father's eyes on me, and that was quite enough. I put the bread and marge down. I'd apologize. I'd make it up to her. Wrapped in my blanket, I went back to my bedroom. I moved the bed back to its old place. I took the photograph of my parents out of the frame I'd put on my bedside table. I made a pile of my dirty clothes. I retrieved the crucifix from the back of the cupboard where I'd thrown it, and once I was dressed I hung it back on its nail. Madame Bianchotti came in at that moment, carrying her black shopping bag. I was standing on the bed in my socks. She put the shopping bag down.

Her thanks didn't grate on me. I might have a good heart, as Madame Bianchotti said, but she didn't know anything yet! Well, nor did I really, but it was the thought that counted, and my meeting a few days later with Monsieur Rosenberg, the former chairman of the Israelite Friendly Association. He was trying to make a list of people who needed help, offering advice and practical relief.

He asked what I could do.

I looked at him and smiled. 'Play the piano. Decline Latin nouns. But apart from that, not much.'

'Well, listen, David, the Association may be able to help you carry on with your studies and –'

I interrupted him firmly.

'I'm not asking for charity. I'll go back to my studies when my parents are home. I want work, that's all. A job.'

He lowered his head, reluctant to meet my eyes. Then he scratched his ear, an old habit of his before coming to any decision. He wanted to sidetrack me:

he thought about it hard and came up with the ultimate argument.

'But your hands, David! Your parents wanted you to be a pianist.'

'I don't care about my hands. I want to put them to some kind of useful work.'

And I did.

Monsieur Rosenberg, who was a furrier, gave me a job himself. I kept it secret. Madame Bianchotti didn't ask me any questions, even if my present conduct obviously intrigued her. I got up before she did, went out, and came back late, tired but happy. She would be waiting with a frugal meal for me. I'd sit down, eat it, hug her and then go to bed.

For a week, a long week, I toiled away backstitching and overstitching and lining. I kept my temper when I got a rocket. I shrugged it off when Monsieur Rosenberg talked to other people about me in Yiddish, explaining I didn't know what, but I could guess. I was still a 'poor child'. 'And if we don't do something to help him, between us . . . '

His customers brought in their minks and astrakhans to be patched up, and looked pityingly at me. I didn't care. Every stitch I sewed in Monsieur Rosenberg's shop, every coat I slipped on the dummy, was bringing me closer to my parents. When they came home I'd be able to help them. And I worked hard.

'Take a rest, David,' said Monsieur Rosenberg one day. 'I know there's a lot of work to be done in this cold weather, but it doesn't have to be forced labour. Come along and have a cup of tea.'

I drank the tea. Monsieur Rosenberg talked about his wife, and building up the Friendly Association again, and how good life would be after the war. The Germans had retreated to the Ardennes, as we gathered from the radio with its all-day background music of Maurice Chevalier songs.

All I wanted to do was get back to my rabbit-skins, pin them to the board and sew and sew till evening, till I was stupefied.

A stitch for Father. A stitch for Mother.

At the end of the first week I watched Monsieur Rosenberg lower the iron shutter, shook hands with him and hurried off. Madame Bianchotti was waiting for me in the kitchen. The table was laid. Bursting with pleasure, I put my parcel on the table – I'd been careful not to shake it about too much – and without taking my coat off I took all the money Monsieur Rosenberg had given me out of my pocket. My first pay. In cash and in kind.

I went over to Madame Bianchotti, went down on my knees and stammered something along the lines of, 'I'm sorry, and this is for you.' Then I started crying with my head on her lap, while she stroked my hair, not really understanding what it was all about.

I had done what I ought to, and I'd do the same every week, minus the tears once I'd got used to it.

It was good to feel the old lady's hands on my head, a forgotten warmth coming back. A long, slow ebbing of despair, no pain or remorse, just a sense of being alive.

I got up. I didn't feel ashamed. I took my coat off and very carefully opened the parcel. Six eggs, a packet of genuine coffee, and some butter, real butter like butter before the war.

I produced them all in turn. Madame Bianchotti came over to look at these simple things. They made her cry. She stroked the eggs, one by one. The happiness of the past clung to those small items. Who would once have thought that an egg, a little butter and some coffee could ever make a person weep for joy?

Suddenly I saw alarm in her face. She couldn't help saying, 'Oh, you didn't steal them, did you? Promise?'

I smiled. She smiled back and then apologized, stroking the eggs again.

As we ate an omelette I told her my secret.

Before I went to bed, Madame Bianchotti had restored my pride to me. 'Your parents would be so proud of you, David!' she said.

Every week brought extra rations. The day I put a chicken down on the table Madame Bianchotti turned pale and had to hold on to her chair. Once she felt calmer she sat down, sadly.

'To think we're reduced to this, David! The black market. People making money out of other poor folk, when we ought all to be helping each other.'

I sprang to Monsieur Rosenberg's defence.

'It's nothing to do with him,' she said. 'There are traffickers in everything, people who've made fortunes during the war, and they're still at it. A disgrace to our country, they are. I'm sometimes ashamed to be French. Can you understand that?'

I couldn't, not really. Nor her growing anger.

'It's not the way I was brought up! It's immoral. Disgraceful. They've even brought me down to their own level. We're like dogs fighting for a bone. I happily exchange my litre of wine, which I don't like, for coupons to buy a couple of kilos of bread.'

'It won't last much longer,' I told her. 'You just wait. Anyway, the Americans are sending us food now. I heard about it this afternoon. Whole boat-loads of food.'

'I know. I know it won't last. But meanwhile we've lent ourselves to unworthy, unforgivable practices. Jesus Christ . . . '

She stopped herself in mid-flow.

'Well, we can talk about that some other time, David. You'll be getting up early tomorrow.'

A person who is going to get up early is supposed to have been asleep first, but sleep eluded me that night. The sandman must have gone on the black market too.

I'd been sleeping for six months now in a bed that wasn't my own, and a room that wasn't my own, and still the war didn't finally come to an end. I had paid a few hesitant visits to the cinema. I'd watched the newsreels, showing the bombing of Dresden. I wanted my parents back; that was all I asked.

I shall never know just why that particular night was so dreadful, as bad as my sleepless night in Monsieur Rigal's house. Maybe it was what Madame Bianchotti had said? I took it personally. I was hand in glove with the black marketeers, since I was ready to accept the shame of it. Maybe – but there are so many maybes. The fact was that I was sitting on the floor with all my worldly goods: Claire's letters, the exercise book I was going to give my parents. My story up to the time I left the empty house was all written down in there. I leafed through it. That was a mistake.

I saw the empty house again, with Lonia, Maurice, Hanna, Perla, the twins, Samuel. They were all talking at once, calling to me for help, and there was nothing I could do, nothing at all.

I spent the entire night tossing and turning, weeping, getting up, punching my pillows, shouting insults at God, France, the French, suddenly calming down and promising myself I'd write to Monsieur Rigal, I'd see Thumper again. Then I'd have another fit of violent emotion, and regret it again. I spent that night going back over almost three years, beginning on an early July morning at the window of this very room. I only just managed to keep myself from breaking it. I didn't mind if I cut my hands and they bled. I'd seen the raid from that window.

Three little knocks at my door told me it was time to get up.

*

An ordinary working day. Monsieur Rosenberg had taught me to use the sewing machine. He was humming at his cutting-out table. But we both knew that this evening would be no ordinary evening.

After dark we walked slowly down the Rue de Paris side by side in silence, not looking at each other. It was a kind of cat-and-mouse game we'd been playing all day, trying to meet one another's eyes, then avoiding them, begging for scraps of comfort. Only a little way now, and we'd have reached the hall where an extraordinary meeting of the Friendly Association was being held. To keep an appointment with absent friends. There were clenched hands, nervous smiles, embraces as people saw their friends again – and there was the silence of death for the dead who had gone for ever.

Sitting in a corner the secretary, Madame Katz, held the roll call, going down the list in her big black notebook.

'Abramovitch?'

'Yes, yes. Here, present!'

All faces were turned towards the chubby-cheeked fat man, an ironmonger from the Place de Villiers.

'Aron?'

No reply.

'Aron?'

'He was picked up during the raid. With his wife and their two children.'

The reply came from Madame Rosen, while Madame Katz entered four question marks in the big black book.

'Berelov?'

'Present.'

'Cohen?'

'Not back yet, but I do have news of them. They wrote to me. They're all still alive down in the country.'

Monsieur Rosenberg suddenly took my hand, squeezing it as hard as he could, as if he didn't want to hear his own name spoken. But my family came before his in alphabetical order.

And two more question marks went down in the black book.

When it came to Monsieur Rosenberg, there was a line to be ruled.

'She died in the Free Zone.'

He had been determined to say it out loud, in a firm voice, before putting his arms round me and starting to cry.

Half an hour of torture. Throats tight, sighs of relief, then more tears, more question marks, more ruled lines.

By the time she got to the Zylbersteins, Madame Katz had only a thread of a voice left. Grown men aren't supposed to cry, but I never saw so many tears.

A few moments of emotion, and then Monsieur Blumenfeld got up on a table and started shouting.

'I told you. I told you so. We ought to have

fought back. We ought to have refused to wear their yellow stars, we never should have trusted them! But you took no notice of anything I said. And here we all are snivelling about it! It's our fault too.'

'So what do you suggest we do now, Mister Know-all, since you're so clever? Are you going to bring the dead back to us?'

A quarrel had started, just the kind my father used to tell me about. Insults were hurled, there were calls to order, people made the quarrel up – all part of life.

'The Zionists were right! Our future is in Israel. A country of our own.'

'Nonsense! France is our country.'

And everyone joined in, in their different accents. A few women, taking refuge at the back of the room, were talking in low voices.

'We must honour our dead, clean up the Jewish area of the cemetery and hold a ceremony there.'

This motion was passed unanimously.

'We must –' We must do this, that and the other. *I* must sit there for over two hours, dazed by claims, counter-claims, proposals, counter-proposals, then questions of 'What are you going to be?' and invitations to 'Drop in on us any time you like'.

Thanks. Thanks, all of you, I thought, but I need to breathe. I suddenly got up and went out into the cold air.

I would wait as long as it took for Madame Katz to rub out those two question marks opposite my surname.

*

Next day Monsieur Rosenberg told me he had been re-elected chairman, and there had been a collection for people like me. He slipped me several banknotes: they came from the aid fund. As if money could make up for missing people! I gave the notes back to him.

'Ah, you're just like your father.'

I wonder if he knew those words meant more to me than all the money in the world?

Other people were too overwhelming. I didn't want to listen to them, or their jokes. 'Well now, David, no girlfriend on the horizon?'

And they would look to see if I blushed, but my face gave nothing away. It was the horizon itself that interested me, the rhythm of the seasons. Summer, autumn, winter, all gone. Spring had come. Mireille the pop singer sang about lying in the hay, with the sun, the sun, for company today. The Russians and Americans had met at the river Elbe, and there were the names of unknown towns in the air, while that other popular singer Charles Trénet sang about the last time he saw Paris, and going home alone, and singing in the rain on the Grands Boulevards and all that. But it was the place names which attracted my attention as I listened to the news. Polish names. German names. The imminent return of our prisoners of war. Hope grew, and so did anxiety. As chairman of the Friendly Association, Monsieur Rosenberg was expected to know everything.

The shop was always full.

'Any more news?'

Monsieur Rosenberg repeated what he had heard on the radio.

'Yes, yes, we know that. You think we don't listen to the radio too?'

Monsieur Rosenberg made a helpless gesture, and then pulled himself together.

'I'll go and find out, all right? I'll let you know the moment I know anything myself.'

One morning I found him waiting for me outside the iron shutter, which was still down.

'Look, David, you take the day off. I couldn't sleep a wink last night. I really must try to get news. I'm sick of looking such a fool.'

And he left me standing on the pavement and marched resolutely off.

A discreet ring at Madame Bianchotti's doorbell. At this time of night? Who could it be? In her dressing gown, she went to undo the three bolts, taking care not to unhook the chain. I was right behind her.

'Oh, it's you! Come along in, do.'

I realized it was something serious. Monsieur Rosenberg's face was waxen, and he was walking with some difficulty. He didn't spare a glance for Madame Bianchotti, who melted tactfully away.

He looked at me, about to speak, but he couldn't bring out the words. He just sat there staring at me. In alarm I went over to him and knelt down.

'Is something wrong?'

He ran his hand through my hair. Making a great effort, drawing a slow, slow breath, he whispered, 'The POWs and Jews – they'll be coming back.'

What wonderful dramatic effect! I jumped up and hugged Monsieur Rosenberg, beside myself for joy. I closed my eyes and clenched my fists, shaking with happiness.

I'd forgotten what a good actor Monsieur Rosenberg was. He always played the clown at the Friendly Association's annual party, unrecognizable in his costume. I let off steam by racing round the dining room.

Monsieur Rosenberg wasn't looking at me. His mind was elsewhere. I wished he'd stop acting now. He'd made his big effect. I waited for his face to clear. It didn't. He really didn't look at all well as he sat there perfectly still.

'You said they'll be coming back!'

He just shrugged his shoulders. I shook him.

'So what is it? What exactly do you know?'

Gently, he took my hand to make me sit down, and placed his own hand on my shoulder. He spoke in a low voice.

'They'll be coming back, yes, we know that, but no one knows exactly who'll be coming back, or how many. And I've heard – I've heard some terrible things.'

He could say no more. He got up and left, and he didn't open the shop next day.

Well, what did that matter, seeing they were

coming back? Madame Bianchotti couldn't have seen me so cheerful since I first came home. Monsieur Rosenberg was obviously shattered, but I was full of great good humour.

'They're coming back, Madame Bianchotti, they're coming back!' I told her.

'Sweet Jesus!' she replied.

I was prepared to embrace her crucifix, jumping up on my bed in my shoes, yelling, 'We've done it! It's all over, it's all over!'

Madame Bianchotti watched me dancing about, and there was no reproachful look in her eyes on account of the bedspread.

They'd be coming back. Quick, quick, I must get everything ready, have the place tidy . . . Gradually my dolphin-like leaps became mere flea-jumps, and then stopped altogether.

Madame Bianchotti had hurried over to make sure I didn't stagger off the bed in my dazed state. She helped me down.

'What is it, David?'

Each leap had been one stage of their return home in my mind. I saw them coming in through the front door. I had everything neat and clean. The floor was polished. All my tired mother had to do was sit down. The kettle was on the boil.

I'd been on the boil too! Now I realized that our flat didn't look like itself at all, and was currently occupied by two loathsome skunks I jostled purposely whenever I met them on the stairs.

The pair of them shattered my imaginary reunion

and all the scenes I was staging.

'You're white as a sheet, David. Sit down.'

Never mind the colour of my face: I must get those bastards out. It was unthinkable for my parents not to come home to their own flat, whatever state it was in.

I had my strength back now, and the urge to violence with it. A few strides and I'd retrieved and loaded my pistol. In a moment or so I'd have our flat back.

It was definitely an unequal combat in Madame Bianchotti's entrance hall. She got there ahead of me and stood with her back to the door, barring my way. A tiny little lady in black. I could have sent her spinning with a flick of my wrist. She'd taken it into her head to stop me in my mad career.

One look was enough to bring me to a halt. There was neither anger nor pity in it. She just said, 'No.' I could do nothing but obey. I turned.

'It's for my parents. They'll be coming back.'

'I know. But no one has the right to take justice for himself, by himself.'

'It's our flat! What will they say when they get back?'

'Never mind that. There are laws.'

That word 'laws' again! She sounded like my father. My imploring voice changed. I was firing words off at random now. 'So you still believe in laws? You mean you've swallowed that one?'

'We are not barbarians, David.'

'You've seen what comes of obeying the law,

though, haven't you? And you still fall for it?'

She hadn't understood anything. Laws are changed at will. The registration of the Jews, the wearing of yellow stars, the confiscation of Jewish property, the raid on my home – all those measures had been carried out in the name of the law.

I held that against her, just as I held it against my father. But I forgave her for her simplicity. Such trustfulness. She believed in France, the land of liberty.

'It's the law, David, and if you respect the law nothing will go wrong.'

What total nonsense!

Nothing will go wrong.

Three years of my life wasted, years in which nothing went wrong? Three years where nothing went wrong for my parents? Three years of sweetness and light? How could Madame Bianchotti be so blind? And I was supposed to be the barbarian, the person who wanted to reclaim his flat after the law had taken it away from him! Because the law had let two vultures sell my parents' things and throw mine out!

I said a lot of coarse things as I tried to make Madame Bianchotti understand and relent, make her let me go and throw them out of our home, by force if necessary.

She didn't weaken.

'The law will turn them out. It will take time. But I won't let you do anything about it. And you know you can all of you stay here while you're waiting.'

I didn't reply. At the great age of sixteen, I knew that laws are made and unmade in the name of the strongest. It's the law of the jungle. Where was the wonderful future Lonia promised us? Where was her world of justice and brotherhood? And where were my parents?

I put the pistol down on the table. I was beaten. Madame Bianchotti picked it up and took it into her bedroom.

'I'll get rid of that tomorrow.'

She could do what she liked. I didn't care. I was right, though.

She left me defeated, my head resting on my forearm, exhausted after fighting and losing a battle.

But others had lost the war, and a good thing too. *Le Figaro* had printed a picture of the bodies of Mussolini and his mistress on public view after their execution. It was horrible: they were hung up by the feet. Madame Bianchotti had done her best to keep me from looking at the photograph, fearing it might shock my sensitive nature.

Dear Madame Bianchotti. And dear Monsieur Rosenberg, who had lived through the exodus from Poland, but lacked the imagination to envisage true horror.

'Go on, David, take a day off, ' he told me. 'Take as many as you like. Don't worry, I'm sure they'll be coming back.'

But it seemed that Monsieur Rosenberg wouldn't look me in the eye any more. His voice was broken. He was very bad at keeping secrets.

The heat of May became unbearable, and so did the waiting. I couldn't just stay at Madame Bianchotti's, moving from my bedroom to the dining room, from the kitchen back to bed again.

And they were coming back; they really were. More and more of them every day. They arrived at the Gare du Nord and the Gare de l'Est. It was a scrimmage, badly controlled by a few superannuated policemen who tried to bar the way to the platforms. The place was swarming with women and children they'd dragged along, squalling kids with arms almost wrenched out of their sockets as an announcement from a hissing loudspeaker set off a rush. Red Cross nurses, all smiles, answered questions they'd been too busy elsewhere to hear properly. Lines of prisoners, bearded or shaven, clean or dirty, happy or sad, passed in front of me. It made me feel quite dizzy.

Prisoners of war coming back had nothing to do with me. My mother hadn't been a soldier, had she?

But the others would be coming, and I went back to the railway stations too. I saw the same embraces daily, the same tears, the same laughter, the same grief. Still no sign of my parents. Perhaps we'd just missed each other? I hurried to the Métro, raced home to Madame Bianchotti. They weren't there. It had to start all over again. The comings and goings, the Gare du Nord, the Gare de l'Est.

I felt helpless, and I also had a dull sense of fear fed by a few words I picked up in passing during the hours of impatient waiting.

'No, he's all right, but I hear others aren't.'

'I caught sight of some weird-looking people at one point. You'd have thought they were corpses, but they were walking.'

Enigmatic phrases, trumpeted out loud in the happiness of reunion.

Suppose those others, the 'weird-looking people', were my parents? Perhaps Monsieur Rosenberg knew. He looked so sad. But he himself had told me they'd be coming back.

'He must be thinking of his wife,' said Madame Bianchotti, by way of explanation.

More waiting. The rollercoaster of hope. And my envy.

I wished I was the little boy of six I saw at the Gare du Nord, his hair well combed, in tears while his mother tried to cheer him up.

'You surely aren't crying when you're going to see your daddy? Oh, stop it, do, you big silly! Your daddy! Just think how pleased he's going to be to see you, too!'

A sniff. 'What's my daddy look like?'

'Come on, they're announcing his train. Dry your eyes.'

I'd have rushed to meet that train, but the stupid child was digging his heels in. Reunions took place on the end of that platform. But it was a desert to me.

In the evening, after the disappointment, came the surreptitious waiting.

Up on the fourth floor, with the window wide open to let the mild air in, I leaned on the sill with Madame Bianchotti beside me. We might have been grandmother and grandson. Dependent on charity, bent on keeping alive, looking out at the little street of the present and thinking of the past. We kept long silences. I sometimes felt a kind of savage mockery, and I was always angry when I saw the heads of that wretched couple from the second floor go by. Suppose I spat on them? What good would it do?

The paving stones used to barricade the corner of the Rue Garibaldi and the Rue François Arago had been replaced after a fashion. The local bar was always full, and Madame Bianchotti narrowed her lips at the raucous laughter rising from it. I could read her disapproval in her face, and she could read the sadness in my eyes as I looked at Monsieur Armellino's abandoned shop with its broken glass canopy.

She placed her hand on mine. Nothing had changed. A few children were playing hopscotch; the top and bottom squares in the French version of the game are marked Heaven and Earth. It was a case of Paradise or Hell so far as I was concerned. Superstitiously, I watched the tin can the kids were throwing into the squares.

Long ago, playing myself, I used to give it a little push with my foot, laughing, while my mother and father watched indulgently. I gave them a little wave of my hand and then forgot about them until night was falling, and I heard the shout of 'David!'

which brought me back indoors to them and their love.

Madame Lenoir had put her chair out on the pavement opposite. She was knitting. The dirty children of the Cour des Miracles kept pestering those few passers-by who ventured to stop by the huge gateway, with rows of huts made of planks and corrugated iron behind it.

Courtyard of Miracles! Ho, ho! But suppose a miracle really did happen?

Abruptly, I turned to look at the far end of the Rue Marceau. I imagined them coming along it slowly, suitcases in their hands. They were looking up at the window on the fourth floor. I waved. I raced downstairs.

But it was getting dark. Madame Bianchotti sighed. She closed the window. Another night. Another day to wait.

And as day followed day I realized that people were lying to me. Monsieur Rosenberg knew something. Well, I didn't care what it did to him, he was going to tell me his secret. I didn't go to either of the railway stations, I gave up that lark and went straight to his shop.

This was the slack season. He was alone at his cutting-out table.

'I'm sick of all this, Monsieur Rosenberg!' I shouted. 'You know! You do know something, but you're not telling me. It's only soldiers who are coming home. What about the others? My parents and all the other people *they* took?'

'Listen, David –'

'I won't listen to anything but the truth. Where are they? What's become of them? You know. You've been to all the Jewish reunions. I'm sorry. I know you're feeling unhappy, but I don't mind. I'm feeling unhappy myself.'

I snatched up a pair of scissors.

'And if you won't talk, I can tell you you'd better watch out!'

Monsieur Rosenberg was not at all alarmed. He dropped his rabbit-skins. 'Put those away and sit down,' he said.

The sewing machine stood between us. He fiddled with the lever working the presser foot, and a squeal broke the silence of the May morning.

'Auschwitz. Dachau. Bergen-Belsen. Dora. Mauthausen. Do those names mean anything to you?'

'No.'

'They didn't mean anything to me either, not until these last few days. Well, listen. Listen hard. I'm sorry if it upsets you as much as it's upset me, but anyway I don't think I can cope with keeping this to myself any longer.'

I listened. I learned of the existence of the concentration camps, the extermination camps, and the fate of the Jews in them.

Monsieur Rosenberg told me only what he knew. Some people would not come back because the Nazis had killed them. It seemed that the Allies had seen some dreadful sights when they liberated those camps. It seemed that the survivors were like living corpses, but they were gradually coming back now. Arriving at the Lutétia Hotel.

'What, the hotel where the Germans were stationed?'

'Yes. In the Boulevard Raspail.'

I stood up.

'Oh, be careful, David, it's terrible. I'll come with you. Just let me get my jacket on.'

'No. I can manage on my own.'

What could be so terrible about it if they were coming back?

On the wooden seat in the underground train, my head leaning against the window, all Monsieur Rosenberg had said flew out of my mind. I hadn't fully understood the things he was telling me. They were just words without explanations. Names which meant nothing to me. And saying something was 'terrible' didn't convey much more.

'Terrible' ought to have been replaced by some word that doesn't even exist.

When I got out of the Métro at Sèvres-Babylone station, I found a crowd that had suddenly fallen silent watching the arrival of a coach. I watched too. What could be more commonplace? And what could have been more terrifying than the look of the women who came out of it, wearing striped pyjamas, supported or carried out, or managing to walk into the hotel lounge by themselves? A silence fell, deeper than any I'd ever known. Skeleton women. Women with eyes fixed on another, unknown world, looking at us blankly. I felt blank too. There wasn't a cry, not so much as a 'Why?' or a 'How?' Only a sob occasionally escaping from the crowd as it moved aside. Shaven skulls, skulls with scarves over them, but most of all, those eyes.

My father had lied to me. He said that, given a dictionary, you can describe everything you see and feel. That's not true. There just weren't enough words in the dictionary for this, and there was no one to invent them. No words to say what can't be said.

I have only inadequate, everyday words to say that, at that moment, I knew Maurice, Hanna, Samuel and little Perla would never come back.

Supposing my mother was among these women, how would I even recognize her? She wouldn't have her blue, gentle gaze any more, she'd have eyes like these, returning from some unspeakable other place.

Monsieur Rosenberg had been right to keep quiet. He too must have seen those 'displaced persons', as they were called, coming back like corpses dug up from the grave.

Once they had all gone into the hotel, words came back, and cries and tears. The crowd in its own turn surged in after them. One man fainted.

All I could see of the lounge was a vast scrimmage, with thousands of photographs pinned to walls, and tables where volunteer workers sat looking at lists and saying, 'No', 'Not yet', or 'I don't know'.

I went out to get some air, dived down into the Métro and hurried back to collapse on my bed. I shed tears which weren't even a relief any more. And then I imagined my father's face as he bent over me when I was a small child, telling me about the pogroms, even brave enough to tell me how a gang of anti-Semitic Poles had strangled his first wife Rachel, and his other children Isaac, Elias and Sarah, born long before me.

Well, I can be brave enough to tell my own tale too.

I took the photograph of my parents and went back to the Lutétia Hotel, day after day, to face its horrors. People kept saying, 'I don't know. You must wait.' So I waited.

I walked down corridors. Without bothering to knock, I opened the doors of rooms where nurses were looking after patients who were dead, or very nearly. I showed the old picture of my mother and father in their best clothes to blank eyes.

Then, briefly, one glance lit up. The man looked at me. He made a sign to his wife, who was sitting beside the bed, and murmured something. She rose, wrote her name and address on a piece of paper and gave it to me.

'Come and see us the day after tomorrow. That's when my husband's being discharged.'

Hope on a page torn out of a notebook.

Hope in their bedroom. Monsieur Brenner was in bed. He signed to me to sit down beside him.

There was no emotion in his voice.

'Show me that photo again.'

I held it out to him.

'Yes, it's them. Grunbaum, Jacob and Clara. I was with them at Drancy, and when they crammed us all into cattle trucks. Your father, he kept on saying we must do something, we weren't animals, we had to stand up to them. No one would listen to him. Your mother calmed him down, but he was like a madman. He wanted to fight. When they made us get out at the camp he had no strength left. He didn't mind about anyone. He just went for the first German he saw and tried to strangle him. Your mother ran up, and then there was a burst of machine-gun fire. I helped carry them away. He was a real *Mensch*, your father, he was a good person. You can be proud of him.'

He gave me back the photograph.

I stayed there sitting on Monsieur Brenner's bed for a long time, holding his fleshless hand. I had no one to wait for now.

And Madame Katz, secretary of the Friendly Association, neatly ruled a line through my parents' names in her big black notebook.

Author's Note on the Lutétia Hotel

In June 1940 the Abwehr, the intelligence and counter-espionage service of the Wehrmacht, the German army, took over the premises of the Lutétia Hotel, which had been requisitioned by the occupying forces. The hotel was also to provide accommodation for certain high-ranking German officers: Admiral Canaris, the head of the Abwehr, moved into it.

At the time of the Liberation the Lutétia Hotel became a repatriation centre: a great many deportees passed through it. Volunteers recorded their identities to assist in people's search for their relatives, and provided initial nursing care.

There were many who, like David, entered the place with mingled hope and fear, to pin up the photograph of a loved one in the huge hotel lounge, beside hundreds and hundreds of other such photographs . . .